"Did you miss me or something?" he whispered.

The baby blinked up at him, then her eyes drifted shut once more. Bryce couldn't help but feel a little smug about her preference for him. He'd kind of missed her, too, if he had to admit to it.

Lily stood at the stove scooping cookies off the pan with a spatula and depositing them onto a plate. She was beautiful—even more so when she was focused on a job she enjoyed, like this one. He could see her happiness in the way she held herself, the way her shoulders were squared and the way her eyes shone.

Stop enjoying this, he told himself gruffly. *This isn't yours.*

The baby in his arms, the beautiful woman across the kitchen, the family arguing at the table—none of this was his. It was tempting in a way he'd never felt before, but it was firmly out of reach. And he'd best remember it. This was a closed door.

Patricia Johns writes from Alberta, Canada. She has her Hon. BA in English literature and currently writes for Harlequin's Love Inspired, Western Romance and Heartwarming lines. You can find her at patriciajohnsromance.com.

Books by Patricia Johns

Love Inspired

Comfort Creek Lawmen

Deputy Daddy

His Unexpected Family
The Rancher's City Girl
A Firefighter's Promise
The Lawman's Surprise Family

Harlequin Heartwarming

A Baxter's Redemption

Harlequin Western Romance

Hope, Montana

Safe in the Lawman's Arms
Her Stubborn Cowboy
The Cowboy's Christmas Bride
The Cowboy's Valentine Bride
The Triplets' Cowboy Daddy

Deputy Daddy

Patricia Johns

HARLEQUIN® LOVE INSPIRED®

LOVE INSPIRED BOOKS

Recycling programs for this product may not exist in your area.

ISBN-13: 978-0-373-62288-7

Deputy Daddy

www.Harlequin.com

Printed In U.S.A.

A father to the fatherless, a defender of widows... God sets the lonely in families.
—*Psalms* 68:5–6

To my husband, who inspires all this romance.

And to our little boy, who *really* wanted Mom to dedicate a book to him, too.

You are my everything!

Chapter One

❧

"You'll need to burp her after that bottle," Police Chief Chance Morgan said, glancing over his shoulder on his way past Bryce Camden's temporary desk.

Bryce looked down at the tiny baby in the crook of his arm. She barely seemed to weigh anything, her rump resting in the palm of his hand and her tiny hands opening and closing in the rhythm of her drinking. The small Colorado town of Comfort Creek was the remote location of his disciplinary action for having punched a fellow officer in the kisser. He'd arrived that morning with an angry simmer in the pit of his stomach that barely covered the sour taste of humiliation, and the police chief dropped a newborn in his lap.

He'd never burped a baby in his life.

"Is that an order, sir?" Bryce asked.

"Yes." The chief shot him an amused look. "Consider this part of your sensitivity training."

The baby had been abandoned at the station in the wee hours of the morning, an out-of-date car seat left on the doorstep. Whoever had left her had pounded on the door and slipped away. When Bryce clocked in for the start of this two-week debacle, they'd immediately put him on baby duty.

So far, sensitivity training looked a whole lot like babysitting, and he'd never been very comfortable around kids, something he had in common with his dad. Some things were hereditary, like the combination of black hair and blue eyes. He was confident that his discomfort with kids came from the same genetic source. His father had been a lousy parent, and he had it on good authority—from his overworked and chronically frustrated mother—that he was just like his old man. And if anyone wanted confirmation on that, they could ask the officer with the split lip.

Christian cops weren't supposed to go around venting their anger with their fists, no matter how good their reasons, and while he'd never been the preachy type, his faith was pretty common knowledge. On Sunday mornings when he was on shift, he'd stand in uniform at the back of his local church and listen to the sermon from there, his radio dialed down to a whisper. So there were certain expectations when it came to him. When anyone else on the force messed up, there was a well of commiseration. They were all human, and a badge and a gun didn't change that. But when the Christian cop messed up, there was a little more judgment, a little more surprise. He'd let them all down.

For the last few hours, Bryce had been calling the baby "Piglet." It just seemed to suit the little thing, and as she drank the last dregs of the bottle, he was forced to stand by the nickname. She released the nipple with a pop and he put the bottle onto the desk, then lifted her gingerly. He'd already been schooled on supporting the downy head, and when he tipped her forward onto his chest, she squirmed again and let out a little whimper of protest.

"Okay—" Bryce patted at the tiny back tentatively. "How do I do this exactly?"

The last few burpings and diaper changes had been taken over by some officers who had kids, so they knew the ropes when it came to infants. Now it was his turn, and no one seemed to pity him. He heard the front door open and close behind him as he attempted to position the baby on his shoulder.

A female voice said, "Where is the baby now?"

He heaved a sigh of relief. Reinforcements were here. That was probably the promised foster care provider. He patted the baby's back gently, afraid of pummeling the infant too hard. In response, she let out a resounding burp.

"Nice one, Piglet," he congratulated the infant, and he turned to see who would be relieving him of his duty when he stopped short.

She wasn't the matronly type that he had anticipated. This woman was young with short-cropped blond hair that swept over her forehead and brought out her big blue eyes. She had a smattering of freckles over her nose, too, that struck him as sweet. A white sundress patterned with stemmed cherries swung around her knees, and she wore a pair of low sling-back heels that completed her feminine look.

"Just over here," the police chief said. "This is Officer Bryce Camden. He's here in Comfort Creek for a short time."

There was a depth of meaning behind those words, and the young woman regarded him with one arched brow. Did she know what that meant—that he was here completing disciplinary action? He gave her a curt nod. "Nice to meet you."

"You, too. I'm Lily Ellison—your temporary foster care." Her eyes crinkled when she smiled, and her face was transformed from pretty to stunning. "Now, who do we have here?"

"No name provided," the chief said with a shake of his head. "I suppose you could do the honors, Lily."

Lily leaned closer to Bryce, a delicate fragrance of vanilla wafting around him momentarily as she slipped the infant out of his arms. Her skin was silky as it brushed against his when she took the baby, obviously more practiced than he was. She smiled down into the baby's face. "Hi there, cutie. You need a name."

Lily stood next to Bryce, so close that her skirt brushed his pant leg where he sat at the desk he'd been assigned for the next couple of weeks. A bottle, a cloth and a few diapers sat on the desktop next to him, and he wondered if he should gather them up for her, but he wasn't sure where she'd even put them, so he left them where they were.

"What have you been calling her?" Lily asked, glanced down at Bryce.

"I've been calling her Piglet."

She rolled her eyes. "That's awful."

"Wait till you see her go to town on a bottle," he retorted.

"How about Emily? If I ever have a little girl, I want to name her that, so I could share it, I suppose." Lily looked down at the baby again. "Little Emily. Does that suit you?"

When the police chief headed off toward his office to grab the paperwork, Bryce eyed her speculatively.

"You look really young for this," he said.

"For what?" she asked, brushing some hair out of her eyes.

"Foster care. Normally foster moms are—" he paused, uncertain how to say this delicately "—more mature."

In his experience, foster moms were a tough lot of women—they had to be. Sometimes they had raised large families of their own, and they'd seen a lot, been through the wringer with the system more than once. They knew what troubled kids looked like, and their big hearts took thorough beatings.

"I've helped raise four younger brothers," she said. "I'm qualified. Trust me."

"Four." He joked, "I'm sorry. That sounds painful."

Her expression melted into a more relaxed smile. "You think you're funny, but you haven't met my brothers. So, you're Bryce Camden?"

"That's right."

"You're staying at my bed-and-breakfast." She turned her attention back to the baby, although her words were meant for him. "Two weeks, paid in full. You're my first guest, actually. I assume you're arriving tonight after work?"

Bryce's mind went back to the phone conversation he'd had with the owner of Comfort Creek B and B when he'd been irritably setting up his living arrangements for his stay. It had been a hurried discussion, but the B and B was pretty much the only place to stay in Comfort Creek, except for a dumpy-looking hotel that the department would have paid for, but the rebel in him wanted at least a small part of this on his own terms. He'd never imagined that the woman on the other end of that phone call was as pretty as this, or that he'd have to explain too much about his reasons for being here. "Yeah, I'll be coming by after my shift is done."

The police chief sauntered back to Bryce's desk with a clipboard, and as he had Lily sign the necessary paperwork, Bryce looked at the baby once more. She had fallen asleep in Lily's arms, her rosebud mouth still moving in a sucking motion. While he'd done his best not to bond with the infant, he had a feeling that he'd miss her.

"I'll see you later," Lily said, handing the clipboard back to the chief. She shot Bryce a smile. "I have your room ready. I think you'll be very comfortable."

There was no way to politely get out of this tonight. He'd just have to make the best of it. Right now, he was sincerely regretting having paid for the full two weeks up front. Staying with the town's temporary foster care wasn't a great idea.

"Thanks," he said. "Do you need this stuff?"

"Please."

Chief Morgan passed him a plastic bag, and Bryce gathered up the various baby accoutrements from his desk and put them inside. When he handed the bag to Lily, her hand lingered under his for a moment, and he met her clear gaze. Long lashes fringed her blue eyes, and for a moment he found all of his thoughts draining from his head.

"I'll see you this evening," she said. "For a nominal fee, I include dinners, too. Tonight would be chicken fettuccini."

"That sounds great," he said, which it did, but this still wasn't a great plan. One night at the B and B with a decent dinner wouldn't kill him, though. It would sure beat eating at that local burger joint that would effectively clog his arteries by the end of his time in Comfort Creek. It might be an acceptable risk, given the circumstances. "Oh, I should mention—she likes 'America the Beautiful.'"

"Like, as a lullaby?"

"Yeah. I didn't know what else to sing to her, and it worked. So—" he shrugged "—heads up on that."

"We'll muddle through." She cast him a smile, then turned toward the door. He'd just have to find a way out of the rest of the stay, because baby care wasn't his strong suit, and Lily Ellison was too charming for his own good. He was here to do his time and get out. Period.

Lily peeked into the bassinet where little Emily lay in the corner of the spacious kitchen. Lily had been surprised when Chief Morgan called and asked if she could stand in as temporary foster care, and for a moment she'd considered turning him down. She had her first guest checking in today—a much-needed start to paying off some of this debt she'd accrued in renovating the old house. But she'd gotten her foster parent certification for a reason: she loved kids, and their town needed a backup to the one foster family it already had.

Growing up, her brothers had been like a tornado, and keeping up with their antics had been difficult. She'd gone from child to babysitter overnight, and she'd never had the luxury of messing up. The boys, however, ran roughshod over every rule or limit she put up for them. They'd eaten all the food in the house, devoured any treat their mother might have scrounged for the kids, occupied every spare inch that Lily might have been able to use for herself. And instead of terrorizing them back, she'd grudgingly let them have the bag of cookies, the TV time, the kitchen, the living room, the bathroom, their mother's attention...because she loved them. And while foster care wouldn't be easy, she had enough experience with rowdy, difficult kids that she felt like she had something to contribute. Every kid deserved love.

But when she started her business, she'd decided to put foster parenting on hold. She was finally fulfilling a lifelong dream of owning her own bed-and-breakfast, and that would require her whole attention. Then, of course, there was Aunt Clarisse's wedding coming up—more family obligation—and her plate was officially full.

But hearing that the child was a newborn baby girl, her heart had melted. How much trouble could a tiny little girl be? The houseful of boys has been a noisy stampede, but she'd always wished for another girl in the family—someone to appreciate the feminine things with her. Her mother had been too busy with work and the boys for that. Lily was assured that this was a temporary arrangement, and she agreed. Her freedom would have to wait until Beverly Starchuck, the regular foster care provider, returned to Comfort Creek.

The kitchen was large, using up a full half of the main floor of the house. An old-fashioned stove and refrigerator dominated one side of the room, and a counter island sat squarely in the center, copper pots and pans hanging down from ceiling hooks above. A pot of thick Alfredo sauce sat cooling on the back burner of the stove, a colander of noodles draining in the oversize sink. This evening, the side door was propped open with a rock, revealing the wraparound veranda, and a warm, fragrant breeze swept inside.

Her guest would be here any minute now. Bryce Camden reminded her too much of her little brothers—good-looking, filled with testosterone and probably far more trouble than he was worth. Obviously, a first impression didn't go too far, but she knew exactly why police officers came for two-week visits to their out-of-the-way town, and that was for disciplinary action. Bryce was no different from the others, and she'd had her fill of rebellious and charming men. Her little brothers had made certain of that. Now she had her sights set on one goal: some freedom to focus on her small business. She'd earned it.

Yet she *had* noticed his ice-blue eyes and the way one side of his mouth turned up before the other when he was about to smile. The prospect of having him as her first guest was mildly unsettling. Ironically, she was grateful for a bit of distraction now—Baby Emily and her Aunt Clarisse's upcoming wedding. The entire extended family was in a tizzy about that wedding, and as maid of honor, she'd have her hands full. This was probably the first time she felt thankful for the unending burden of family obligation.

The cheerful chime of the doorbell echoed through the house, and Lily took one last look into the bassinet before heading down the hallway to the front door. Everything was guest-ready—everything, that is, except the flutter in her stomach.

"This is it," she murmured to herself. This was the start of Comfort Creek's Bed-and-Breakfast—her first guest.

When she pulled open the front door, Bryce stood

there with a suitcase in hand, giving her a tentative smile. His uniform fit him perfectly, the two-toned blue bringing out those unsettlingly light eyes. He'd parked a black pickup truck in the shade of a spreading elm tree in the drive.

"You're here," she said, stepping back and holding the door open. "Welcome! I hope you enjoy your stay."

Bryce stepped inside, and she saw him look around the foyer. She knew exactly what he'd be seeing. A hall chest sat against one wall, a beveled mirror hanging above it. A mason jar of lilacs from the side of the house sat on the top of the hall chest, spilling their fragrance around the entranceway. Behind her, a bright white staircase led upstairs.

"Nice place," Bryce said. "A far cry from that hotel along the highway."

"The Melody Inn?" Lily swung the door shut. "That place has a rat infestation. And that isn't just a competitor being catty, either. They're shut down for the next two weeks while they get it under control. They're as big as raccoons, apparently. It's the most interesting thing happening in town right now, besides my Aunt Clarisse's wedding, that is."

Bryce winced. "Well, good thing I'm here, then."

There was something in his voice that gave her pause, and she mentally kicked herself. She had a bad habit of saying too much. This wasn't a friend dropping by for a visit—she was supposed to be professional. Just then the baby started to cry.

"That would be Emily."

She headed back into the kitchen, too aware of the tall man behind her. He had a way of making her feel flustered in spite of herself. She heard Bryce set his suitcase by the door, then his footsteps came down the hallway after her. Emily's tiny cry wavered from the corner. Lily scooped her up and the weeping stopped immediately. Her little onesie was damp from sweat, and Lily could only imagine that some air would feel nice.

Lily noticed Bryce pause in the doorway, and when he saw the baby, his expression grew softer. "How's she doing?" he asked.

"Good." Lily went closer so that he could see Emily's little squished face. "She's been sleeping and going through a lot of bottles of milk. She loves to be held, this one."

"I'm glad," he said, then cleared his throat. "So do you run this place by yourself?" He stepped back, then poked his head out the side door where a padded wicker chair waited invitingly.

"I do," she said. "Can't afford employees yet."

She was proud of the title of sole owner—one she'd hardly dreamed possible. She would never have been able to save up a down payment to get started on her own, so she'd entered a contest for young entrepreneurs in Colorado with her business plan. She'd won first place—a check just big enough for her down payment on the old house and some supplies. Lily was certain it was an answer to her fervent prayers. A chance to climb out of the poverty she'd grown up in. And when God put an opportunity like this in her lap, she wasn't about to squander it.

"Taking care of this place alone—is that safe?" Bryce pulled his head back inside and fixed her with a steady look. His seriousness was almost comical. What did he expect happened in Comfort Creek, exactly?

Lily laughed. "Of course. I know just about everybody in town, and we're only three blocks from the police station." She was also counting on most of her clientele being officers just like Bryce. Comfort Creek was probably the only town this size that had a regular influx of visitors due to the county's training program.

Bryce smiled ruefully. "Sorry. I'm used to a different pace in Fort Collins."

"Yeah, I imagine." She switched the baby to the other arm, and Emily looked around in that cross-eyed way that newborns had.

"So, if you know everyone in town, any guesses as to the mother of Piglet here?" he asked, reaching out to touch her hand. The baby closed her fingers around his thumb.

Lily made a face. "A little piece of advice—never call a girl Piglet." Bryce shot her a teasing grin, a little too much like her brothers did. "And no, I don't know who the mother is. Maybe someone from an outlying community? I have no idea."

She paused. Professionalism must prevail.

"Would you like me to show you to your room?" Lily asked. "Maybe you'd like to get settled before dinner."

"I'm starving, actually. Wouldn't mind eating first," he said.

Lily gestured toward the rustic table, which she had set and ready for dinner. She looked down at the baby and back to Bryce. She couldn't serve food one-handed.

"Hold her, would you? I just need to get dinner off the stove."

Bryce froze for a moment, then awkwardly reached out to accept Emily from her hands. For a man who'd cared for the baby the entire morning, he was certainly acting strange. She eyed him curiously as she served up a heaping plate of fettuccine Alfredo, topping it with strips of lemon-marinated chicken breast. He settled Emily into the crook of his muscular arm, and she looked quickly away. He was a good-looking man, but she didn't feel comfortable noticing that right now.

"So what do you normally do in Fort Collins?" she asked.

"Well, I don't babysit," he said. "There is a lot more actual crime-stopping."

Lily rolled her eyes. "Welcome to Comfort Creek. So what did you do to get sent here?"

She caught a look of embarrassment cross his face, and she immediately regretted the question—at least the phrasing. She was still rather curious about why he was here. What had he done to merit two weeks in the dullest town in Colorado?

"I had a little disagreement with another officer," he said, smiling wanly. "It got…heated."

"Ah." She was curious what "heated" looked like, but she wouldn't ask. Bryce Camden was a big man with a broad chest and muscles that strained his shirtsleeves when he bent his arms. She could imagine that he'd be intimidating.

She brought his plate back to the table and set it in front of him. A jug of pink lemonade sat within his reach, the clear glass fogged with condensation.

"Aren't you eating?" he asked.

"I've already eaten," she admitted. She hadn't worked out how she'd feed her guests—leaving them be or sitting with them. Bryce seemed to want company, so she sat down in a chair opposite him.

"Let me take her back," Lily said, and lifted the baby from his arms. Child care was tiring, but there was something so sweet about little Emily that Lily found herself feeling strangely complete with the baby back in her arms. This hadn't been part of her plan at all, but this tiny girl had her by the heartstrings already.

"So tell me about this aunt's wedding," he said, pouring a glass of lemonade.

"Pardon me?"

"You said it's the most interesting thing happening around here," he said. "Besides rats."

Lily smiled and shook her head. "Well, Aunt Clarisse is widowed. She's about sixty-four or so now. My uncle died ten years ago, and she's been alone all this time. Then all of a sudden she announced that she's getting married to some fellow she met online."

"Oh yeah?" He sat back in his chair and shot her a curious glance. "How long did they date?"

"She says it was for a few months, but we'd never seen him before—or heard of him, for that matter. Last month, Aaron moved to town, and they started planning their wedding." She nodded to his untouched plate of food. "Bon appétit."

"This looks delicious." Bryce bowed his head for a moment, then sank his fork into the noodles without missing a beat. "So what's the problem with Aaron?"

"I didn't say there was a problem," she said with a small smile.

"You didn't need to. You don't hide your feelings very well."

She never had been able to mask her true emotions. But when it came to Aaron, it wasn't that Lily thought that a difference in age was that big of a deal. She'd watched enough crime shows to know that mature widows were a prime target for con men, however—a sentiment shared by half of her extended family.

"He's quite a bit younger than she is," she said.

"How much younger?"

"About twenty years."

"It's not unheard of," Bryce agreed thoughtfully. "But I see the concern."

"So you're right, we're worried."

"Who's we?" he asked, swallowing a bite.

"About half the family," she admitted.

"And the other half?"

"Thinks she's making a fool of herself."

Bryce barked out a laugh. "So you get a feeling that something is up, do you?"

Lily sighed. "If there were something suspicious going on, I'd never forgive myself if I didn't try to protect my aunt. I know that TV isn't real life, but I've seen the shows, and—"

"No, you're right about it looking a bit suspicious. I mean, there might be nothing to it. It might be that two perfectly nice people fell in love with each other and want to get married. A few months of dating is quick, but not unheard of. Like you said, though, you've never seen the guy before. People can pretend to be something they aren't pretty easily online."

"So you think I'm right?" she clarified.

"I think it's worth looking into," he replied, spearing a piece of chicken. "This is amazing, by the way."

"Thank you." Lily smiled at the compliment. She was relieved to have Bryce agreeing with her about her aunt's beau. When she'd mentioned it to another officer she knew, he'd told her that there was no legal obstacle to her aunt marrying anyone she chose. But Officer Nick Colburn had also been fighting with his girlfriend's family at the time, so that might have colored his view a little bit. But if Bryce would help her—

"So, will you look into it, then?" Lily asked.

"Pardon me?" Bryce blinked.

"My aunt's fiancé." She leaned forward. "Will you make sure that he isn't some sort of con man?"

Bryce didn't answer for a moment, and his gaze turned toward the window. Outside there were some fruit trees and a wooden framed swing. He didn't seem to be taking in the scenery, though. Had she overstepped again? Probably. She was the queen of overstepping, it seemed.

"I'm sorry." She rose to her feet and swayed gently, the baby's eyes slowly closing as she did so. "I can get too friendly. I'm used to knowing everyone and—"

"So what's this guy's name?" Bryce asked.

"Are you saying you'll look into it for me?" She stopped rocking, and Emily's eyes popped back open again.

"I might as well," he said. "While I'm here."

Lily blinked back a mist of unexpected emotion and gave a curt nod. She was more relieved than she realized.

"His name is Aaron Bay. He claims to be from Denver. And the wedding is in two weeks, so—"

"So we're on a bit of a tight schedule," Bryce concluded.

"Yes." She smiled. "Thank you, Bryce. You have no idea how grateful I am."

If this officer would help her to get some answers, it would take away one of her worries. Aunt Clarisse was a kind woman—maybe too kind for her own good. A cynical cop was just what they all needed, and his visit was perfectly timed. He had two weeks in town, and she had two weeks until her aunt's wedding.

Lily began to rock Emily again, and those little eyes drooped shut. She might be the queen of overstepping, but she'd keep a tight rein on her behavior with this handsome cop. The last thing she needed was to complicate her life any more than it already was.

Chapter Two

The room smelled faintly of floor polish mingled with the scent of the flowers on the bedside table. His hostess had thought of every detail, from the Wi-Fi password in a silver picture frame to the handmade quilt draped across the end of the bed. Bryce lay between crisp white sheets that smelled ever so subtly of bleach, knowing that he'd probably never been more comfortable in his life, but was still unable to sleep. There was something about the quiet that was throwing him off. How did people relax in a place so ridiculously silent?

Lily and the baby stayed in a little cottage in the back—a structure that probably used to be a mother-in-law suite, but that seemed to serve her purposes nicely. She got some privacy, but she was still close enough if her guests needed anything during the night. She'd given him a phone number for her cell phone and told him not to hesitate to call if he needed anything at all. Truthfully, he'd hesitate. He never had been comfortable being waited on.

Bryce's Bible lay to the side. He'd tried reading it twice already and been unsuccessful.

Lord, I'm sorry.

Bryce wasn't one to shirk the consequences of his own actions, and he knew he'd been wrong when he punched Leroy Higgins. He wasn't the kind of guy to just lose control like that, and the episode had scared him a bit. Leroy had been ragging on him for weeks when he'd found out who his father was.

Bryce's dad had been a police officer, too, until he quit under some fierce allegations of professional misconduct. And while Leroy thought his jokes were hilarious, Bryce had finally had enough. But physically lashing out…that had been wrong and a lot more like his father than he was comfortable with.

Outside an owl hooted, forcing him to take back his last thought about silence. It wasn't completely quiet, really, because there were sounds, just not the kind that he was used to. The constant hum of traffic and the far-off chug of a train did the trick back in Fort Collins. A mystery novel and a couple of Psalms just before turning in had been a great relaxer as well, but all this quiet made his ordinary routines insufficient. His conscience wasn't helping matters, either.

That evening, he'd held Emily for an hour or more while Lily went around cleaning up the kitchen. The baby cried in the bassinet and cried in Lily's arms. The only quiet they managed to get was when he paced the kitchen with Emily snuggled against his chest. What was a guy supposed to do? Lily had cleaned and scrubbed while he paced, and while she worked, she talked. For as much as she talked, though, he had a feeling there was a lot she held back.

Lily was pretty in a way that he didn't see too often in the city. Her hair was natural—not the bottle blond he saw so often. She wore very little makeup, and he was glad of that because the smattering of freckles over her face was endearing. She was petite and slim, but she wasn't weak by any stretch. He'd seen her effortlessly lift a twenty-four-pound bag of flour. It was impressive.

And the whole time he'd held little Emily with those big brown eyes and the black hair that sprang off the top of her head like fireworks. Every time he looked down at that pink bow of a mouth, or let her grasp his finger with that tiny little hand, he couldn't quite forget that he was terrible at this—he had a rotten track record.

There had been other kids in his life, and he'd managed to bungle those relationships. One Christmas Eve, he'd spilled the truth about Santa Claus at his cousin's house. He still felt slightly wronged in that one, though, because he'd had no idea that kids actually still believed in Santa. He never had as a child, and no one had given him the memo about retaining the innocence or whatever. After that he'd stayed away during the holiday, and gave the kids Christmas cards with twenty-dollar bills enclosed. As far as he knew, they were happy with that arrangement—his cousin included.

Then there was the time that he tried to pull the tooth of his partner's youngest daughter. That tooth had been dangling by a thread for the longest time, and he thought if he just gave it a tug…only it didn't come out. The poor girl had hollered and cried and bled into a tissue, and he'd felt like a complete jerk. He hadn't meant to hurt her, and while her parents had been very forgiving and gracious about the whole thing, he still hadn't forgiven himself for that one.

There was a whole litany of stories where Bryce muddled things up with kids—he was no good at it, and he shouldn't be surprised. His dad had been the least comforting, most awkward man when it came to being a father, and Bryce had inherited every last bit of it.

So as he'd cradled Piglet, he tried to pull his emotions away. But whenever he did, Emily would seem to sense a change in him, and she'd start to cry, and he'd be pulled right back into singing "America the Beautiful." And Lily would look at him like he was ridiculous, and he'd know that this arrangement that left him on baby duty was most definitely not working.

He knew it wasn't, but he didn't have a whole lot of choice. It was this or sleeping in his truck, and he knew that he'd be an idiot to give up the clean, cozy bedroom. Somehow, he'd just have to get through these next two weeks, and then escape back to Fort Collins. At least doing a background check on Lily's aunt's fiancé would help to distract him. Besides the beautiful Miss Ellison, Comfort Creek seemed to offer very little distraction from his own personal issues. Perhaps that was part of the strategy out here.

Outside, a different kind of sound broke the night stillness. It was the thump of feet hitting the ground and a soft grunt, followed quickly by another pair of feet and a male voice muttering in irritation. Bryce tossed back the sheet and swung his legs over the edge of the bed. A digital clock glowed 11:00, and Bryce almost rolled his eyes. It felt like the middle of the night here in Comfort Creek. In Fort Collins, he'd be up watching the news.

Bryce crept to the gabled window and looked out. He had a clear view of the yard in the silvery moonlight, and he could see two young men standing in the flower garden, picking their way out of it. They'd obviously just jumped a fence, and they were moving toward the house.

This was the kind of thing he knew how to handle. Babies—not so much. Break-and-enters, trespassers, and general run-of-the-mill bad guys? That was his comfort zone.

Bryce slipped his gun holster over his shoulder and buckled it into place. He slid into a pair of jeans, too. Taking down a couple of perps in pajama bottoms just seemed undignified. His bare feet made no sound on the wooden floorboards as he crept from his bedroom and down the stairs. Everything was silent and still— nothing out of order, but he could hear the muttered voices of the young men outside the kitchen window.

"…give me a boost…"

"Ouch. No, this way—"

Bryce unlocked the side door with a soft *click*, then swung it slowly open. The hinges were well oiled, much to his relief, and he slipped out onto the veranda, then jumped over the railing into the dew-laden grass. The cottage, located down a stone path and no more than fifty feet away, was dark and silent, and he peeked around the side of the house to see the two teenagers attempting to use a crowbar on the window. He rolled his eyes. They were obviously new at this.

"Hey, there," Bryce said conversationally, and both young men startled. The crowbar fell with a *thunk* to the ground and they started moving backward.

"I wouldn't do that if I were you," Bryce said. "I'm faster."

At those words, they took off toward the fence

they'd jumped to get into the yard. If they'd gone in opposite directions, he would have had to choose which one to take down, but since they hadn't thought that far ahead, it didn't take much for Bryce to sprint across the yard and catch them by their shirts halfway up the fence. He jerked them backward and they came down to the ground in a sprawling, wiry mess. Bryce got his knee solidly into the back of one of them, and grabbed the other by an ankle.

"Freeze!" he barked, his tone sharp and cold.

Both young men stopped moving immediately, except for the quick rise and fall of their chests.

Just then, a light came on in the cottage and Lily's face appeared in the window. She disappeared and a moment later appeared in the doorway.

"Burke and Randy, what do you think you're doing?" she demanded.

"You know these two?" Bryce asked incredulously.

"Of course I know them!" she retorted. "These are my little brothers. Two of them, at least. Now answer me!"

The demand was obviously focused on the young men in his grasp. He released them, and they both rose their feet, rubbing at sore spots from the tussle.

"Hey, Lily," the bigger one said. "Didn't mean to wake you up."

"Get in here!" she snapped, then disappeared from the doorway.

Randy and Burke looked at each other sheepishly, then back at Bryce.

"That hurt," the smaller one said resentfully.

"Probably did," Bryce replied, unaffected. "Next time don't run from a cop."

"How were we supposed to know you were a cop?" the bigger one retorted.

Bryce pulled out his badge, then tucked it back into his pocket. "There's your proof."

"Man..." The young men headed toward the cottage where Lily was waiting for them, arms crossed over her chest. She wore a thick bathrobe, closed all the way up to her chin, and her eyes glittered in anger.

"Inside!" she ordered, and Burke and Randy did as they were told. Bryce felt a bit of an urge to obey, too. She sounded an awful lot like his third grade teacher, the memory of whom still struck fear in his heart. When Lily saw Bryce, she rolled her eyes.

"My idiot brothers," she said, shaking her head. "They still think everything I own belongs to them, too."

Bryce followed Lily into the tiny cottage. It seemed to consist of a sitting room, a bathroom—which he could see because the door hung open—and a bedroom to which the door was shut. It was cozy enough, and a tiny cry came through the bedroom door.

"So what are you doing here?" Lily snapped. She shook her head and whipped around. She disappeared into the bedroom and emerged with Emily in her arms.

Burke shuffled his feet against the hardwood floor. "We were hungry. Just came for a snack."

"You've been drinking," she said, shaking her head. "Not only are you underage, but you know full well we have alcoholics in our family. You're playing with fire!"

"Oh, stop the lectures, Lily," Randy said with an exaggerated sigh. "You're worse than Mom!"

"And you're dumber than I thought!" she snapped.

"So this seemed like a good idea…lurking around my yard?"

She picked up a bottle of formula and looked from the baby to the boys, as if undecided on how to balance the three of them. She seemed to make a decision, because she brought both bottle and baby to Bryce, then turned back to her brothers.

"They were breaking in, actually," Bryce said, adjusting the baby in his arms. "They were working at the kitchen window with a crowbar."

Emily wriggled, turning her face toward him, her mouth open in a little circle. She let out a whimper, hands grasping at the air. He'd given Emily a bottle at the precinct, so he knew how this worked at least, and he popped it into her mouth. She settled in, slurping hungrily.

"Breaking in?" Lily's eyebrows shot up and stared at her brothers incredulously. "You were trying to break in to *raid my fridge*?"

Both young men shrugged. "Nothing in the fridge at home."

Lily glanced toward Bryce, and they exchanged a look. Emily wriggled in his arms, and he looked down at the baby—Emily's needs not pausing even for a second while they tried to deal with Lily's brothers. Why couldn't babies come preprogrammed with patience?

Bryce wasn't sure that he even believed them that they were here for food. If they had addiction issues at this age, they'd also be accomplished liars. A drug test would shed the light pretty quickly. Lily, however, seemed to believe them.

"Did it ever occur to you that Mom might need some help?" she demanded. "Randy, you're sixteen, and Burke, you could have gotten a job last year. If you worked this summer, you could give Mom a bit toward groceries. What makes you think that you're owed everything?"

"Come on, Lily. You're our sister."

"Do you have any idea how much it would cost to fix that window after you broke it open?" she demanded.

"You've got a customer coming soon. Charge him extra."

"Officer Camden here is my guest for the next two weeks," she said through gritted teeth. Her eyes flashed in anger, but she seemed to be trying to keep it under control.

"Oh." Both looked Bryce. "We thought—"

"You thought what, exactly?" Lily's tone turned dangerous. "I don't care what you see on TV, you should know better than to assume that about *me*." The boys looked sheepish, and Lily shook her head. "I have half a mind to drag you to church with me this Sunday and get your heads on straight. The next time you come into my house without first being invited inside, I will press charges."

"What?" Burke looked offended. "So now we aren't welcome here?"

"You are not welcome to climb through my windows!" Lily closed her eyes, then sighed. "Consider this a warning, boys. If you did this to anyone else, you'd be getting yourselves a criminal record. This is mine. My home. My life. My business. Hands off!"

"Fine," Randy muttered sarcastically. "Nice to know you care."

"I do care." She marched over to a closet, wrenched it open and pulled out four boxes of cereal. Apparently,

Lily also used her cottage for extra pantry storage. "I, more than anyone else in this town, care for you, and enough to make sure you don't land yourself in jail one of these days for being utter morons." Her eyes flashed fury, and she shoved the cereal boxes into their hands. "I'll bring by some groceries tomorrow, but if I ever catch you drinking again—"

When Lily told him that she'd raised four little brothers, he'd had a cuter mental image than this one. These young men were out of control, and while Lily seemed to believe that all they wanted was a snack, he highly doubted it. If they were willing to break into their sister's house, then he suspected they'd be willing to walk off with something they could sell for extra cash. He was more cynical when it came to people's criminal capabilities.

Five minutes later, Lily's brothers were gone, the baby had finished her bottle, and Lily had sunk into a chair by the window, looking tired.

"Did you want some tea?" Lily asked. "I could go over to the house and put on a kettle."

"No." Bryce fixed her with a direct stare. "I don't need looking after. I want to know what that was."

"My brothers."

"Yeah, apparently," he said with a shake of his head. "How often have they done this before?"

"I didn't have the doors locked before," she said with a sigh. "But with a guest, I obviously can't have my brothers coming and going like they own the place."

So maybe there was a chance that this was a food run, after all. He was having trouble garnering any respect for the young men, though. They obviously felt completely entitled to everything that their sister had worked for.

"She needs to be burped," Lily said, grabbing a cloth and putting it over her shoulder. Bryce lifted the baby, and as she came upright, she let out a wet burp that dribbled down his wrist and onto the floor.

"Oh, that must feel better," Lily crooned, taking the baby from him and putting her up onto her shoulder, where she continued to pat her back. "Let me get you a cloth, Bryce."

She cast him a humored smile while he stared down at the dribbling mess. This was most definitely gross, and he'd seen a lot in his career.

"They aren't bad boys," Lily went on, passing him a cloth. "They're angry. They're lonely. They—" She shrugged. "They treat me like a second mother half the time. My dad died just after the youngest were born— they're twins—so I pitched in and took over at home while my mom worked to keep us fed. It turned into an odd dynamic."

Bryce wiped his arm, then the floor, his mind going back to his own father. His dad had left when he was six—a cocky police officer who ruffled his son's hair and said, *Don't worry, Bryce. I'll be around.* Famous last words, because he saw his father only a few times a year after that, and Bryce and his mother had been left to figure it out together.

"My dad was out of the picture pretty early, too," Bryce said. "You do what you have to."

"Well, I didn't do it well enough, if they turned out like this." She turned sad eyes toward the window as if she could see them in her mind's eye.

"You were a kid yourself."

She smiled wanly. "I suppose."

"You were right, though, that they'll end up with a criminal record that way," he said.

"I know." She met his gaze frankly. "And I'm worried about them."

If she gave an inch, those boys would take over everything she'd worked for. Bryce could see that clearly enough—just as clearly as he could see that she loved them quite ferociously.

"Don't feel bad about having your own life," he said.

"I don't." She rubbed gentle circles onto the baby's back, and from Bryce's position, he could see that Emily was asleep again. "I want my freedom. I want my own life. I want to take care of me, and only me, and not have to think about everyone who needs something from me all the time."

"And foster care?" It didn't seem to fit into that description.

"I'm only the backup foster care around here," she said, "but even so, I'm supposed to be taking some time away from it all."

He could understand that. She'd obviously been in the role of caregiver ever since she was a kid. Kids never did a very good job of raising each other. He didn't blame their mother, and he didn't blame Lily. They'd done the best they could after a death.

"Is that selfish?" she asked.

"Nope." He cast her a smile.

Lily moved Emily and looked down into her sleeping face. "I've wanted to run a B and B since I was a kid, and I want to do this on my own."

"Freedom," he said.

"Freedom." A smile spread over her face, and a

glimmer of light came back into her eyes. "I've been holding out for this since I turned eighteen, and I thought I'd finally gotten it."

Lily looked up at the clock on the wall, and Bryce's eyes followed hers. It was nearly midnight.

"I'd better get the baby back to bed," she said. "I'm really sorry about tonight."

"I know." He grinned. "Those Yelp reviews can be brutal."

Lily rolled her eyes. "You aren't half as funny as you think you are, Bryce." She paused, grimaced. "Please don't mention this on Yelp."

"I was joking." He caught her eye. "I promise. Have a good night. I'll lock up over in the house."

She gave him a tired smile, and he went to the door.

"Emily really likes you," she said softly, and Bryce turned back. Lily cradled the baby in her arms, and somehow when she was cuddling the infant, everything about her looked softer. She was beautiful in a way that went right down to the core, and it warmed a place in his heart that he wasn't comfortable peeking into. He wasn't good for kids. He wasn't a family man. He was a good cop, and he was a good man deep down, but he knew where to draw the line.

"You're going to have to teach her to have better taste in men," he said wryly, then turned back to the door. "Good night, Lily."

Lily deserved her taste of freedom, and while he didn't know if it was even possible, he'd like to be the one to break her out.

The next day, Lily stood in the guest room Bryce was occupying, pulling the sheets from the bed. Her mind was on the episode from the night before, her stomach clenched in anxiety. He was a cop—a cop! And her brothers had tried to break into the house where he was sleeping. She was grateful he hadn't arrested them on the spot and brought them into the station. She was even more grateful he hadn't pressed charges.

Not that they didn't deserve it. That was the worst part. She tore the bottom sheet from the mattress and wadded it into a ball. This could have been the start of a criminal record for each. They were still her little brothers, and the thought of them facing authorities was enough to bring tears to her eyes.

"Stupid, stupid, stupid," she muttered. Why did the boys have to ignore every piece of advice she gave them? Why couldn't they see the consequences waiting for them? And while she'd thought that a B and B would be a great idea for this town to house the visiting officers, last night she realized exactly what she'd done—set up her own brothers' eventual arrests if she couldn't get them straightened out.

She definitely needed to step back from any foster parenting—her hands were already full with the boys. What good was she to the kids who'd move through her home if she couldn't be the same stable influence for her own brothers? Family was supposed to come first.

Bryce's suitcase lay on one chair, zipped shut. If it weren't for that bag, she would hardly have seen any evidence of him being here. She looked at it for a moment, pushing back the temptation to snoop. She wasn't a snoop by nature—it was that little rebellious streak inside her that constantly wondered *What if I just...*

When her boyfriend had asked her to move to Denver with him three years ago, it was *What if I just left? What if I started a whole new life in a big city?* But even then, she knew enough to realize that if she walked away, she couldn't live with the consequences of how it would affect the lives of her little brothers.

She'd been praying all morning that God would show her how to protect those boys, from everything… including the cop under her roof. It was crazy to think of an officer of the law as the enemy, because she'd always been a friend of the police force. But this was about her brothers, and her protective instincts superseded anything else. Maybe if they grew up a little more…maturity might make a difference. Randy and Burke were sixteen and fifteen respectively, and the twins were only thirteen. None of the boys were terribly mature yet.

And Bryce was kindly helping her look into Aaron Bay. A good thing—she knew that! But that also pulled him in closer to her personal life, and that included her brothers. She'd set this whole thing up, and she felt trapped.

After her brothers left, she'd gone back to bed, but she'd been woken up twice by a very hungry little Emily. And as she looked around this room, she wished that she could be more focused on her business. She'd wanted this for so long, and she was deeply proud of this house, the decor, her careful plans to make sure her guests had as pleasant a stay as possible, and she regretted being unable to focus on it completely. But with everything that was happening around here, she just couldn't.

In fact, she'd just gotten off the phone with her aunt, who'd been gushing over honeymoon plans. Apparently, they wanted to go to Europe—a perfectly romantic-sounding trip, except that Lily's first thought was that her aunt would be off American soil, which felt more vulnerable. Lily knew she was trying to protect all of them, but was she strong enough to pull it off?

She flapped a sheet over the mattress, and it came down in a white billow. As she tucked the corners in tightly, she remembered all her daydreams as she got ready to open her bed-and-breakfast. None of them had included all the other drama. Her vision of owning her own business had included her being able to focus on the running of it without constant interruption. She'd imagined herself doing laundry, cooking meals, making up the perfect brunch for her guests, picking apples from the trees out back to make homemade pies—

Okay, it was possible that her daydreams had been slightly idealized… She hadn't anticipated how much real life would creep in, though. She'd wanted some freedom, but when you loved people as deeply as she loved her family, maybe that kind of independence wasn't possible.

Lily flapped the next sheet over the bed and tucked it in with efficient swipes. She pulled a wrapped chocolate out of her apron pocket and deposited it onto the pillow, then grabbed the jar of flowers off the bedside table. She'd bring up some fresh ones later on.

The doorbell rang, and Lily trotted down the stairs to open the door. She glanced into her sitting room where Emily slept, then came to the front door and pulled it open.

Bryce stood on the doorstep. He'd arrived in a police minivan. Her heart skipped a beat—a cop on her doorstep…just like she'd feared. She looked around him at the unimpressive vehicle.

"Since I'm only here for a couple of weeks, they assigned me the loser cruiser," Bryce said with a grin.

Lily laughed, pushing back her anxiety. This was her job—this was her guest. She could only take care of what was in front of her.

"As a guest here, you don't have to ring the bell, you know," she said.

"Didn't want to be mistaken for your brothers." He shot her a teasing grin. "You looked like you could have done damage."

If only he could forget about her brothers. "Are you hungry?"

"Not really." He stepped inside. "I did do a little digging for you, though."

"Oh?" Lily's curiosity flared up at those words. She wasn't sure what she'd hoped for, but some answers about her aunt's fiancé would be a bigger relief than he probably realized. She led the way to the kitchen, where she tossed the old flowers into the garbage and put the mason jar in the sink. She turned back toward Bryce. "What did you find?"

"Good news and bad news." He paused, that little smile toying at his lips again. "The good news is that he has absolutely no criminal record. No outstanding warrants."

"That's a relief." Maybe she'd been worrying for nothing, after all.

"He also has no tickets or driving infractions."

"Okay." Was Bryce just rubbing it in now? "I guess we were wrong. That's a good thing. Thanks for looking into it."

She turned on the water and rinsed out the jar, then put it onto the dish rack to dry. Bryce didn't say anything else until she turned again and saw him watching her, arms crossed over his chest.

"The bad news is that he's most definitely not who he claims to be. He doesn't have much of a government paper trail at all." Bryce's voice was low and soft. "He has a credit history that's about ten years old. Anything before that is a black hole. He has a driver's license—again, obtained ten years ago. No birth certificate. I can dig some more, though. I could find out what ID he used to get the driver's license here."

Lily turned this information over in her mind slowly. How did a person go through life without leaving much of a trail? She personally had all sorts of proof of her existence, from parking tickets to the mortgage on this house. A person put their signature down so many times during a lifetime, even in order to move into another state, that it seemed impossible to have no paper trail fated further back than ten years. Obviously something happened ten years ago.

"There are about two hundred Aaron Bays in the United States right now, so investigating could take some time." He gave her an apologetic smile.

"So, what's he hiding?"

"Hard to tell without a little more digging," he said. "And now I'm curious. There is definitely something up."

Lily nodded. It looked like her suspicions had been right, after all. It was one thing to imagine the worst, and quite another to have her worry supported by a police officer.

"I should add, though," Bryce said, "while I'm looking into this, it would be best not to tell anyone else about it. If we come up with a perfectly logical explanation for it all, and in the meantime we've turned your entire family against the guy—"

Lily nodded and leaned back against the sink. "That's a good point." Her mind went back to her aunt's invitation to dinner tonight. She'd turned her down, saying that she had a lodger and couldn't get away, but an idea was percolating. It was risky—it would pull him in closer to her family matters, but it could also distract him from her brothers, and possibly give them all the answers they needed before this wedding.

"How would you like to see him in person tonight?"

Bryce raised an eyebrow. "How would you pull that off?"

"My aunt asked me to dinner so she could see Emily." She shrugged. "What self-respecting aunt doesn't want to snuggle a baby?"

"Wouldn't it be a little strange for me to come along?"

It would, she had to admit. But if Bryce were more than a friend, his presence would be explained easily enough.

"We could take our chances on that," she said. "We'll tell them that you're my first guest and that I'm terrible with professional boundaries. Which is entirely true."

Bryce was silent for a moment, and she wondered if she'd overstepped once more. Then he nodded, humor sparking in his eyes.

"Yeah, that would be good. I'm curious to sit down with the guy."

"So should I tell her that we'll be there?" she asked.

Bryce turned toward the doorway of the kitchen, then paused and looked back at her.

"Sure," he said with a nod. "I've got a meeting with the chief in about fifteen minutes, so I should head out." A smile twitched at the corners of his lips. "I have to say—my stay in your town isn't turning out to be anything like I expected."

It wasn't anything like she'd imagined, either.

"We're like that around here," she replied. "Welcome to Comfort Creek."

Chapter Three

Bryce was used to driving a regular police cruiser, and being in the "loser cruiser" made him feel like a kid with a dunce cap. He wasn't here to do any real police work—and that point was made clear by the minivan. No one would take him seriously in this thing.

I can survive anything for two weeks, he reminded himself.

The discipline was the embarrassing part of this. He didn't need to learn his lesson about not lashing out. He knew that full well, and he was going to make sure it never happened again. He didn't need the attitude adjustment, so coming out here like one of the department's problem officers stung. His dad had been a problem officer, and he wondered if this chastisement was because of the shadow his father had cast. Like father, like son, right?

He glanced at his watch. He was due to be in a meeting with the chief in about ten minutes. Today, the "book work" portion of his sensitivity training started. He wasn't looking forward to this. This was the place where they outlined for him in painful, workbook-filled detail that he shouldn't pummel fellow officers. It was like writing lines in elementary school.

I will not punch idiot coworkers.

I will not punch idiot coworkers.

I will not—

Bryce wouldn't let himself be baited like that again. Part of what made this so humiliating was that Leroy was proving a point—Bryce *was* just like his father. His dad had been disciplined twice for excessive use of force, and in the end they'd found him involved with a couple of other officers who'd been taking bribes. While his father hadn't been caught red-handed, he did resign quite promptly, and the rumors swirled. Richard Camden was a prime example of when good cops go bad, and his reputation was forever tarnished.

If he'd been innocent, why resign? Why not clear his name? By that time, Bryce was already a young officer on the force, and his father's fall from grace had hurt him, too. The thing was, Bryce had hoped that he and his dad could bond over some mutual ground now that they were both cops. He'd hoped that his distant, negligent father would see someone in Bryce he could be proud of at long last, but there hadn't been time for any of that. When his father was disgraced, Bryce lost a last, tenuous connection to his father. Turned out that his dad didn't have a good excuse for his parental absence, after all. And now that Bryce was a cop, and his father was no longer on the force, it only pushed Bryce further away.

The Comfort Creek police station was a quaint little affair, and it reminded Bryce of Mayberry and *The Andy Griffith Show*. The whole town had that feeling about it—like all problems should be able to be solved in twenty-two minutes, and end with some time at a fishing hole. If only real life were so picturesque.

Bryce parked and hopped out into the warm summer sunlight. He stepped over the bulging cracks in the asphalt where the tree roots were barging through, and trotted up the front steps to the station. The receptionist gave him a curt nod as he came inside—obviously she was used to the run of visiting officers and hadn't much time for pleasantries. It was just as well. He was feeling less than pleasant anyway.

He headed toward the chief's office, and when he stopped at the door, Chief Morgan waved him in.

"Good. You're here." He sat behind a desk, typing away at something, and only glanced up for a moment.

"Hi, Chief," Bryce said.

The chief motioned for him to close the door and turned back to his computer. Bryce sat down in the chair opposite and waited. The rattle of keys filled the room, and Bryce glanced around. There were a few pictures of the chief with a yellow Labrador retriever, but that was it for personal effects. There were a couple diplomas on the wall, an award or two, a picture of the chief in full uniform next to a portly-looking fellow— a mayor, maybe? He looked official. The smile didn't seem to make it to either man's eyes.

"Okay." Chief Morgan hit the last button on his keyboard and turned toward Bryce. "So today we start the more in-depth part of your training."

Bryce tried to look appropriately interested. "I'm ready, sir."

"Great." The chief leaned back in his chair. "So tell me about this fight."

"It was stupid, sir. Nothing to tell."

"Do you tend to hit other officers for no reason at all?" he inquired, arching one brow.

"Not normally, sir."

"So there was more to this, then." The chief looked at him evenly. "Because I've looked at your record, and you're generally a good officer. You work hard. You take extra shifts. You hand in your paperwork on time, and besides being late a few times, your history is good."

It was in direct contrast to his father's track record, and while Bryce had been proud of his clean slate, there had been a small part of him—the boy inside—who worried that it would only push him further away from his dad. What would it take to get an "atta boy" from his old man?

"Thanks for that, sir."

"So what's the deal, then?"

Bryce sighed. "It was a low blow, sir. Officer Higgins had been pestering me about a personal matter for weeks, and one day after a long shift when I was tired, I snapped."

"Hmm." Chief Morgan nodded slowly. "Do you know that I know your father?"

Bryce felt the blood drain from his face, and he attempted to keep his composure, but he wasn't sure how successful he was. He cleared his throat and looked away.

"I'm not my old man, sir." Bryce glanced back at the chief irritably. "With all due respect."

"Your father is the reason I'm the cop I am today," the chief went on. "I worked for a few months in Fort Collins before I was able to get a position here at home. He was my first partner, and he showed me the ropes.

We kept up with each other over the years. He wasn't a conventional cop, but I don't think he was dirty. If he'd been guilty of taking bribes, he'd have been charged."

Bryce tried to hide his surprise. It was a small county, apparently, and this was the last place he'd think to look for someone who actually sided with his dad.

"Looks like you saw more of him than I did, sir," Bryce replied.

Silence stretched between them, but Bryce could read sympathy on the chief's face.

"I said he was a good partner, not a good father," the chief said quietly. "There's a difference."

This was getting way more personal than he was comfortable with. "I'd rather not talk about it, if it's all the same to you."

"He called me," Chief Morgan said.

Bryce suppressed a wince. So after all this time his father decided to take an interest in him? Great timing.

"What did he want?" Bryce asked warily. Somehow that made it worse, having his father know about his failure. Or was this a silver lining—something in common at long last? He didn't want it this way. He'd never dreamed of bonding with his dad at rock bottom.

"He asked me to go easy on you."

Bryce barked out a laugh. "This isn't exactly Guantanamo Bay!"

"That's pretty close to what I said." The chief laughed softly. "The thing is, good officers climb and climb, and sometimes the pressure gets to be too much. They burn out. They make a bad choice, and then they topple from their pedestal."

"Yeah, I get it," Bryce said drily. "I'm just like my

old man. I'm a good officer who made a dumb choice. Maybe I should forgive my father for his twenty-odd years of shortcomings."

Chief Morgan ignored the dripping sarcasm and shrugged. "Forgive him or not, I don't really care. And I didn't say you were like him."

"Then what are you getting at?" Bryce demanded. "Because this is pretty personal here."

"I know that Officer Higgins had been needling you about your father," Chief Morgan said.

"Oh." So that little nugget had been passed along, too, had it? He might have opened with that and saved them this delightful back-and-forth.

"And I think that when you make your peace with your father's failure, you'll be a better officer."

Bryce clenched his teeth and looked away. So now Chief Morgan was going to play shrink with him? Since when did his personal issues with his old man have anything to do with his ability to do his job? It was one mistake to hit Higgins, and everyone was treating him like some sort of ticking time bomb, ready to go at any moment. He was professional. He was thorough. He did his job, and when he clocked out at the end of the day, if he held a few resentments against the father who abandoned him, it was no one else's business.

"You disagree?" Chief Morgan asked.

"I do." Bryce shook his head. "I imagine you've got a few personal issues of your own, Chief. Every man has them, but it doesn't make it the business of the precinct."

"It is if it affects your ability to be a good cop," came the reply. "You carry a badge and a gun. You'd better have your personal demons well in hand."

The chief opened his desk drawer and pulled out a small notebook. He tossed it across the desk toward Bryce.

"What's this?" Bryce asked.

"A notebook." The chief nodded toward it. "I want you to write down every time you pretend to be something you're not."

"Excuse me?" Who didn't pretend to be something they weren't from time to time? Every man did it, from pretending to be stronger than he was to pretending not to feel things. That was the male experience. Men weren't allowed to be scared. They weren't allowed to cry. They kept tough. They proved their fathers wrong.

"That's your assignment," the chief said. "Write down every time you pretend to be something you're not."

"I heard you the first time," Bryce said. "But that's a little ridiculous, isn't it? We do that constantly in this job. We have to look tougher than we are. We have an image to maintain. We don't show fear, we show confidence."

"Then you should fill it up pretty fast," the chief said with a smile.

"And if I refuse?" Bryce asked.

"You're well within your rights," the chief said with a nod. "If you don't want to do it my way, then you can do it Larimer County's way. I have a room filled with training binders all about feelings and appropriate responses to them. You could get started today, and I'm pretty sure you could work through about fifteen to twenty of them by the end of your time here."

That was playing dirty. Bryce could do it the chief's

way, or spend his next two weeks hip-deep in procedural training.

"You make a compelling argument, sir," Bryce said. He reached for the little notebook and tucked it into his pocket. "We'll do it your way."

"Glad to hear it." The chief shot him a grin. "You'll be patrolling in town with the other officers, and we'll sit down and discuss the list you've written in a few days. Have a good day, Officer Camden."

The chief turned away, and Bryce rose to his feet. That was it? He waited for a moment to see if the chief would say anything more, but he didn't look up again. Bryce walked to the door and opened it, then looked back.

"Say, Chief?" he said.

"Yes?" Chief Morgan looked up.

"If I'm going to be on patrol, what do you say about assigning me a better vehicle?"

Chief Morgan narrowed his eyes in thought, then slowly shook his head. "Sorry, can't do it."

"No other cars available?" Bryce asked.

"No, I have three in the parking lot, but this is good for you. It'll give you a bit of a jump on your assignment there."

Bryce bit back the retort that flew to his lips and shook his head.

"All right. Thanks anyway, sir."

He stepped outside the office and was careful not to shut the chief's door too loudly. So driving that ridiculous minivan was part of the game here, was it? Fine. He'd do his time, and when he was done, he'd go back to his regular post and his regular life in Fort Collins.

I can survive anything for two weeks.

* * *

Lily was the kind of woman who spoke her mind and then regretted it later. She'd gone over that conversation with Bryce in her mind thirty times already, and every time she came to the same conclusion: she'd gone too far. Bryce wasn't from Comfort Creek. He wasn't one of them, and she couldn't treat him like he was. While his help was appreciated and his focus on her aunt was far preferable to his focus on her brothers, it was still a huge breach of professionalism, and she regretted that.

That evening, Lily dressed Emily in a sundress she'd been given by a neighbor and wondered if she could fix this. But how? Bryce had agreed to help them look into Aaron—that was worth something. Why, oh why, didn't she think a little more before opening her mouth and telling a relative stranger all of their family business? Except that her brothers had tried to break into the house, and so that hadn't been avoidable, and her aunt…well, she had been preoccupied with Aunt Clarisse, and apparently, Lily talked too much. And that talkative, too-open personality was her bane. She longed to be elegant and self-controlled. She just… wasn't.

Emily's little legs poked out the bottom of her sundress looking as fragile as porcelain. The baby socks she'd been given kept falling off—too big for those newborn feet—and so she decided to forget about them.

The daylight from the window lit up the room, but the veranda blocked the actual rays of sun. She could see the backs of two chairs from the front porch against the window pane, and she paused to look outside onto the expanse of lawn and that towering elm. Bryce's minivan turned into the drive. He probably thought she was insane, but it was too late now.

Emily lay on a blanket on the floor. She looked up at Lily, her big brown eyes trying to focus on her face. She leaned closer to the baby and smiled.

"Hi, sweetie," she crooned. "You look so pretty!"

Emily's arms flailed, and in spite of all the other drama, a wave of affection rose up inside Lily. This little girl was so precious, yet she was starting out her life with so many challenges. The baby was trying to bond—to find out who would protect her—and Lily wasn't her mother. She was temporary foster care. She wasn't the one Emily was supposed to connect with. But how could a newborn not bond with anyone? She had to. And how could Lily stop her own growing affection?

The front door opened, and Bryce's footsteps echoed in the foyer. He appeared at the door to the sitting room.

"You said before not to knock," he said, shooting her a grin. "Are we leaving now, or—"

"Is this crazy?" she asked, picking the baby up and rising to her feet. "I mean…I'm overstepping tonight, aren't I?"

"Oh, totally," he replied, his expression deadpan. "This is positively nuts, but it kind of beats the other things I had planned."

She laughed, then stopped short. "I'm serious, though."

He was joking around, and she was trying to find her footing here.

"Me, too." He shrugged. "Look, I could check into Aaron in a less obvious way, if you want. I don't have to come along. But now that you've given me the heads-up,

I'm definitely going to look into him. Whether this little dinner happens tonight or not. So no pressure."

"Are you comfortable coming along?" she asked.

"I look at it as undercover work." He flashed a grin. "Speaking of which, I'd better get changed. I'll be down in a minute."

Bryce's footsteps moved up the stairs, and she looked down at Emily. How had she gotten herself into all of this? A baby to care for, a wedding to investigate, her brothers picking the worst time imaginable to beg for attention in the most effective way possible… Add to that this handsome officer that she found herself attracted to, and she needed to keep her head on straight.

A few minutes later, Bryce came back down dressed in a pair of jeans and a gray polo shirt.

"So how are your brothers today?" he asked.

What could she say? He already knew too much about the boys.

"They're fine…far as I know." She shook her head. "They aren't normally quite that bad, so I have to apologize—"

"Sure they are," he countered.

Maybe they were, but she didn't like to admit to it, especially to a police officer. She knew how they looked—how they all looked. She saw the boys differently than anyone else did, though. She saw the little round cherub faces that they used to have. She felt her cheeks heat at his directness.

"So we aren't going to politely pretend that everything is hunky-dory?" she asked. "We can't rewind a little bit there and let me have this?"

"Not tonight," he said with a shrug. "I'm not going to judge, though. I used to be a lot like them."

That did help a little bit. She'd called it before— sensed he was just like her brothers on some level. Maybe he'd be less inclined to teach them a lesson legally, or was she being too hopeful there?

"I could see that," she replied.

"Yeah?" He laughed. "Well, I turned out all right—" He paused, grimaced. "Besides being here for disciplinary action, of course. But that's complicated."

"How much like them were you?" she asked cautiously.

"I stole a car…my uncle's. I was arrested for it. My dad—the cop—called my uncle and talked it out with him. He dropped the charges. It was pretty serious. I could have ended up in juvenile hall."

"Ouch." Yes, it sounded like he did understand. "Getting arrested—did it do you any good?"

He was silent for a moment, then shrugged. "It certainly scared me straight."

Lily glanced at the clock on the wall. They'd need to leave soon to get to her aunt's place on time, and this conversation was getting more personal. What was it about Bryce that kept her slipping right back into that unprofessional territory?

"You ready?" he asked.

"I just need to put the car seat into the back of the car," she said. "And I'll drive."

She felt more comfortable driving—it kept her in control, and right now she needed that.

As Lily turned toward the door, her sandaled foot hit something wet on the hardwood floor. Her heel slipped, and her heart flew to her throat. Just as the thought sparked in her mind that she was about to fall, a solid arm shot out and clamped around her rib cage, catching her in one arm, with the other broad hand placed protectively over the baby's back. Bryce pulled her hard against his side, and she could feel the solidness of his ribs against hers.

Lily sucked in a surprised breath and looked up, past that strong shoulder and into Bryce's face, which was now only inches from her own. She could see the roughness of his stubble, the tiny lines around his eyes, and could feel the heat of his breath against her cheek.

"You okay?" His voice was low and warm, and his grip on her loosened as she regained her balance.

"Yes, I'm fine. Thank you." She looked down at the baby, who didn't seemed the least fazed by their near fall.

"Good." He released them then, and her waist felt suddenly cool where his arm had been. She looked over to find his eyes pinned to her, his expression revealing nothing of what he was feeling underneath. She was struck by how quickly he'd moved and by how easily he'd caught her.

She let out a shaky breath.

"Let's go then," she said quickly, unwilling to admit to herself how nice it had been to fall into those strong arms. She couldn't get used to that. He was helpful, he seemed genuine, he was willing to look into Aaron for them…but he was also very temporary, and he knew too much. She should at least try to regain some professional composure with this man. He was her first guest, after all, and she wanted to do this right.

Unfortunately, she was bringing him to a family dinner to investigate her aunt's fiancé. "Doing it right" had pretty much sailed. She might have to start fresh with the next guest, and just accept that things had gotten out of hand with Bryce from the start.

Chapter Four

Even though the baby was in a rear-facing car seat, Bryce kept looking back to check on her. From her silence, he concluded she was sleeping. He didn't have to worry; she was most certainly Lily's job now, but Piglet had snuggled her way into the back of his mind. Maybe it was how he'd met her at the police station, or her clear preference for him his first night at Lily's place, but he still couldn't shake a certain feeling of responsibility for the kid.

"Is she sleeping?" Lily asked.

"I think so."

The sun was low in the sky as they drove down a rural gravel road, the shadows stretching long and slow like taffy. The road ran straight, going up and down unending hills so that they went from golden evening sunlight to chilly shadow, and then back up again. The mailboxes at the end of driveways out here didn't have numbers, they had names: the Wetsteins, the Millgroves, the Burnetts.

Lily leaned back in the driver's seat, comfortable and relaxed. She tugged her fingers through her hair, pulling it away from her eyes, and Bryce looked quickly away. She was pretty in a way that seemed to draw him in—her milky skin, those sky-blue eyes, her long lashes—and he had to keep some firm control on his impulses. He wasn't here to get attached, and just because he'd landed in Lily's B and B with nothing but time on his hands didn't mean that he had the luxury of letting himself feel.

Lily had tried to back off to more professional territory this evening, and he hadn't complied. That had been selfish on his part, but he found himself liking this view into her life. She was tender but tough, and he'd realized that her opening up the way she had was comforting. She was one of the few people who hadn't treated him like a live grenade since he'd punched Leroy.

She obviously didn't need to look for names or numbers to know where she was. Still, it felt a bit odd to be driven somewhere. Back in Fort Collins, Bryce was the one who did the driving. Being single, that stood to reason, but he also drove his mother for errands from time to time, and when he took a woman out, he did the picking up. So he felt awkward in the passenger seat tonight.

Not that he minded. Lily was the kind of woman who didn't seem to want the extra help. She'd struggled getting the baby's car seat strapped into the back, and she'd downright refused any offer of help from him.

"I got it!" she kept calling from the depths of the vehicle whenever he offered a hand. "No, no, I'm good. I got it!"

And eventually, she did get it, so who was he to

complain? But it took a full four minutes. He'd timed it on his watch.

Her aunt's drive was on the left, and it opened up onto a large front yard that appeared to be lined on one side by raspberry bushes. A large tree loomed over the house in the backyard, visible over the roof, but the front yard was open and clear. Two vehicles were parked in front of a sagging garage, and Lily parked behind them.

"Here we are," she said, sucking in a breath. "Aaron comes across as a nice guy. You'll probably like him."

"Feeling guilty?" he asked with a wry smile.

"A little." She winced. "I do hope there's nothing wrong with him. I want to be clear about that. I don't have anything against him personally—"

"I know," he said. "I get it. I'll be discreet. Is that them?"

An older woman came out onto the front porch. She was rounded and short, and wore a fifties-style dress. Her hair was dyed a color that he could only describe as "very brown," and behind her a slim man stood with his hands in his pockets. He had more faded brown hair with a little gray at the temples. His clothes looked faded, too, as if all of him had gone through the wash one too many times.

"That's them," Lily said, and pushed open the door. "Hi, Auntie!" she called.

Bryce got out of the car and came around as Lily pulled open the door to the backseat and crawled in after the car seat.

"Do you want a hand with that?" Aunt Clarisse asked.

"No, she's got it," Bryce said, shooting the older

woman a wry smile. "We've been through this once already."

"Nice to meet you," Clarisse said, leaning forward and giving him a firm handshake. She eyed him speculatively, and Bryce noted the irony here. They'd all be trying to figure one another out tonight, it appeared. "This is Aaron."

The man stepped forward and shook Bryce's hand—his handshake a little weaker than his fiancée's. He smiled and dipped his head in a wordless hello.

Lily emerged with a still-sleeping Emily, and Clarisse paused to heave a breathy sigh over the infant.

"Isn't she sweet…" Clarisse planted a hand over her heart. "Does my heart good! Babies are as good for you as fiber."

Bryce smothered a laugh and exchanged a humored look with Lily. Clarisse didn't look like the kind of woman who needed much rescuing either, and he could see why Lily had such a special bond with her aunt. Besides the difference in their coloring—Lily being fair and blonde next to her aunt's brilliant brunette—he could see a family resemblance. They both carried themselves with a determined forward launch.

"Well, come on in," Clarisse called over her shoulder, and Aaron put an arm around her as they made their way back up the steps and into the house.

Bryce glanced down at Lily, and he could tell that the car seat was heavy. She held it a little away from her body to keep from bumping the sleeping baby, and he reached out and took the handle from her.

"I've got it—" she began, and he flashed her a grin. She released the car seat and smiled gratefully. "Thanks."

"After you," he said, and she stepped in front of him to go through the front door, her floral dress swinging lightly around her calves. He came inside close behind her, and as his eyes adjusted to the indoor lighting, he looked down at the sleeping infant. Emily heaved a tiny sigh in her sleep, and he felt a wave of protectiveness.

He tried to push it off—he shouldn't be feeling this—and as if in an answer to an unsaid prayer, Lily turned and took the car seat from him. He released it quickly and stood back as she unbuckled the straps and lifted the sleeping baby out.

"Oh my…" Clarisse said. "Isn't she precious? I've just got to snuggle this one. There's no getting around it…"

Aaron peeked over Clarisse's shoulder at the baby and smiled. "She's cute, all right."

"Congratulations on the wedding," Bryce said, and Aaron turned toward him.

"Thank you. We're really excited." The other man came across the room to where Bryce stood. "Two weeks and counting now."

"So how did you meet?" he asked.

"Online. We were both on a Christian dating site."

It stood to reason, actually. A lot of people met that way these days. Before Bryce could say anything more, Aaron added, "We weren't exactly clear about your relationship to Lily…"

Was Aaron actually questioning him about his intentions? Bryce couldn't help but smile. Aaron looked innocuous enough, his brow furrowed in mild concern or mild confusion, Bryce couldn't tell which. But mild seemed to describe every inch of this man.

"I'm her boarder for two weeks," Bryce said.

"And she brought you for a family function?" Aaron's pale eyebrows went up. "Clarisse is thinking that you might be something more, and Lily isn't ready to say yet."

Bryce inwardly grimaced. Of course, that was what this looked like, and he was a little embarrassed to have been set on the defensive so quickly by the man he was supposed to be investigating. However, he couldn't let Aaron get suspicious, so he said, "Nothing like that. I'm going to be in town for work reasons for a couple of weeks, and she felt sorry for me. I'm used to a faster pace in the city. She says she's not great with professional boundaries, and here I am."

There was more to it, but the statement was still true. He'd have to put this into his notebook—fakery at its finest.

Aaron met his gaze for a moment, then nodded. "Ah. I see."

Did he see? Bryce glanced across the room to where the women were settled on the sofa. Clarisse had Emily in her arms, and Lily sat with her legs stretched out in front of her, ankles crossed. Lily's gaze flickered up toward him, and she met his look with a smile.

"How has she been sleeping?" Clarisse asked.

"Pretty well," Lily replied. "When she's really fussy, she seems to like Bryce."

"Oh?" Clarisse's eyebrows went up in the same way Aaron's had. "That's very sweet."

"I'll be easily replaced with a pacifier, I'm sure," Bryce said quickly, but as the words came out, his chest constricted a little with regret.

Lord, I have to stop this, he prayed silently. It wasn't a request so much as an acknowledgment of his situation. He wouldn't be here long. But then, in the broader picture, this was temporary for Lily, too, and that baby girl needed someone she could rely on until she had a home. He and Lily would simply have to do—stand-ins until a proper family could be rustled up. Still, getting attached wasn't smart.

Clarisse looked ready to ask more questions, but then she looked down at the baby. "It looks like someone could use a new diaper," she murmured, as if the "someone" in this equation wasn't obvious.

"Here," Lily said with a low laugh. She took the baby back. "I'll take care of it."

"Feel free to use the guest room," Clarisse called after her. Lily disappeared down the hallway, her voice filtering back to them as she crooned to the baby about the state of her diaper with promises for a bright, clean and snuggly future.

It all felt very domestic, and a little too comfortable for Bryce's liking. Obviously, he needed to fit in if he was going to get some useful information out of Aaron, but the lines with Lily seemed to be blurring. Could he blame her—with her questionable ability to keep personal and professional separate? Or was it him—wishing for things he knew he couldn't have? This ridiculously slow town had started to grow on him already.

Bryce noticed the diaper bag at his feet, and he picked it up. "I guess I'd better take this."

Clarisse and Aaron both nodded sagely, and he had the distinct impression that they had the exactly wrong idea of who he was to Lily, and convincing them otherwise wasn't going to be simple. As he headed down the hallway, he touched the notebook in his front pocket.

If this didn't count as pretending to be someone he wasn't, he didn't know what did.

Lily was in a guest bedroom—the second door on the right—and she'd managed to find a towel and had the baby lying on the bed. She looked up in relief as he held up the diaper bag.

"Oh, perfect," she said. "It's been a long time since I've taken care of a baby. I feel out of practice."

"You seem like a pro to me," he said. He pulled out the notebook, clicked his pen, and jotted down,

Pretending I'm not investigating a potential con.

He thought for a moment, then added: *Pretending I know anything at all about baby care.*

He closed the notebook and tucked it back into his pocket.

"What's that?" Lily asked as she set to work on the diaper.

"Part of my punishment," he said drily. "I'm supposed to write down every time I pretend to be something I'm not."

Lily shot him a curious look. "And what did you write down this time?"

He could have added, *Pretending that I don't feel anything for this woman,* but he didn't. Some things weren't the chief's business, and this crush he was developing on the B and B hostess was one of them.

"Oh, baby care," he said, trying to sound offhand. "I'm faking it here."

"Everyone does," she said, pulling another wipe from a plastic package.

"Tell that to the chief," he said wryly.

"So—" She glanced back as she reached for a clean diaper. "What do you think of him?"

"Aaron, you mean?" he asked, lowering his voice. "So far he's the one suspicious of me."

"What?" Lily laughed. "How so?"

"He's convinced I'm here as more than your boarder," he replied. "I kind of threw you under the bus. I used your line that you're terrible with professional boundaries."

Color tinged her cheeks, and she shook her head. "Well, it's true. What can I say? Did it work?"

"Nope." He shot her a grin. "They both still look pretty convinced that I'm your secret beau."

"There are worse rumors to go around, trust me," she said blandly, and she scooped the baby back up and bent at the knees to pick up the diaper and wipes. She turned to face him. "Pick one."

"What?" Bryce looked at her in confusion.

"The baby or the diaper. Take one, would you?"

Given a choice between the two, he chose the baby, and she shot him an amused smile, grabbed the diaper bag, and headed back out of the room. Bryce followed, and he looked down at Piglet in the crook of his arm. Was it his imagination, or had she grown a little bit already?

He could pretend he came from a better family than he did, or that he wasn't too much like his father. In fact, right now he'd really like to pretend that he had a different makeup, different baggage, and that having a family like this was even a possibility. But pretending would only hurt more in the end—it would hurt him when he was forced to face facts, and it would hurt everyone else who would start to rely on him.

Like Lily. Or was it just wishful thinking that she'd

ever entertain those ideas about him? While Piglet was a short-term situation, he could see that mothering came naturally to Lily. She wasn't jaded the way he was. No, it was best to keep all of these lines very firmly drawn. No faking it. The truth might be less attractive, but it was still the truth—he wasn't dad material.

They emerged into the living room once more, and Lily headed off toward the kitchen to find a garbage can, and he nodded at Aaron and Clarisse who turned their attention to him with their curiosity on high beams.

What was it with this town? Comfort Creek just refused to melt into the backdrop of rural Colorado. And two weeks here wasn't going to be quite as forgettable as he'd hoped.

Lily glanced out the window to where the men stood in her aunt's backyard in front of the grill. The backyard was large, a massive maple tree looming over half of it, long limbs spreading luxuriously over the shade-dappled grass. She used to climb that tree as a kid—back when Uncle Earl used to hammer pieces of wood up the side to help them keep their footing. Half the time, one of the uncles would have to come up the tree to help them down again, and Lily had always suspected that those pieces of wood were meant to help the adults more than the kids.

Bryce and Aaron were grilling steaks, the scent of which came wafting inside through the screen door. Bryce's hands were in his pockets, and Aaron stood with a pair of tongs in one hand—master of the grill.

"He's nice," Clarisse said, looking down into Emily's little face. She tugged down the tiny pink dress.

"Aaron does seem very nice," Lily agreed. "I admit that. It's just, how well do you know him after a few months online?"

"I mean Bryce."

Lily whipped around and shot her aunt a wry smile. "Now you're deflecting, Auntie."

Clarisse chuckled. "You still think that Aaron is only with me for my money?" She spread her hands. "This is all I've got—this house. I don't have piles of money in the bank. I have your uncle's pension that keeps body and soul together. If Aaron were after money, he could have found a wealthier woman than me."

"I'm not saying that you aren't a catch." Lily sighed. "I just worry."

"Well, stop worrying. He's a good man, and he loves me. That's not so easy to come by, you know."

Lily nodded and turned back to the salad she was making at the counter. "Don't I know it."

"Which brings us back to Bryce," her aunt said, her tone exaggeratedly casual.

Lily laughed. "It really doesn't."

"I saw the way he was looking at you—"

Lily glanced up. "Oh?" How exactly had Bryce been looking at her? She'd been busy with the baby and her aunt, and she'd assumed that Bryce's attention had been firmly on Aaron—his reason for being here.

"He's smitten."

"He's a boarder!" she exclaimed. "You're imagining this."

"He's *here*." Her aunt raised her eyebrows to make

her point. But her aunt didn't know the real reason why Bryce was here, and it wasn't because of fond feelings for Lily, either. He was doing her a favor and trying to ride out his time here before he headed straight back to his real life in Fort Collins.

"He's a cop, Auntie, and I have four brothers who are out of hand. I don't think that's a great combination right now."

"Oh, you can't let those boys hold you back from living your life," her aunt countered.

"They tried to break into my new place," Lily said. "They were working at my kitchen window with a crowbar. Luckily, Bryce had just arrived and he stopped them before they did too much damage, but still, he's a police officer, and he could have arrested them right there—" Her mind went back to that night, and all those old feelings of resentment, fear and anxiety bubbled up again. "I'm going to try to keep them in line, but I've got my own business now, and I need to focus on it. Do you have any idea how scared I was that Burke and Randy would end up with criminal records?"

Emily squirmed and let out a whimper.

"Trade?" Clarisse suggested, and Lily smiled, holding her arms out for the baby. Clarisse took Lily's place at the counter and reached for some tomatoes. "You deserve your own life, dear. You pitched in after your dad passed, and you did more than anyone could have expected from you, and you've made that old house into something really fine. I'm proud of you."

Lily didn't hear those words often, so they meant something. She'd worked incredibly hard on renovations. She'd done half the work herself, and hired contractors for the rest of it. She'd used up every penny of her award and then some, and while she was pleased with how everything had come together, she wasn't in any position to relax. She was in debt up to her ears, and she needed to start making some money now. But her brothers couldn't grasp that. She'd come into cash, and they figured she should share.

Lily put the baby up onto her shoulder and swung her weight gently from one side to the other. Emily snuggled in against her neck. This baby was such a perfect fresh start—a tiny bundle of squirms and burps, and she couldn't help but wonder what it would be like to raise her as her own. It wasn't fair to even entertain the thought, though. This was why she made terrible temporary foster care—while she had ample experience in taking care of children, she had a lot less experience in letting go.

"I get so tired of taking care of everyone…" Lily felt tears mist her eyes. "I'm so tired, period."

"I know." Clarisse paused in her chopping and gave her niece a tender smile. "It's not easy. That's part of why I took ten years to myself after Earl passed. I was tired."

Her aunt did understand this part all too well. Uncle Earl had been sick for a long time with kidney failure. She'd shuttled him around for dialysis, taken care of him at home, and kept their home around them. Earl had some decent insurance, so she'd been able to be there for him, but for the last six or seven years of their marriage, Clarisse had been dedicated to a sick husband.

"Well, I don't get to just take a break," Lily said with a sigh.

"What if you could?" Clarisse said. "What would you do?"

Lily smiled wistfully. "I'd put in a big garden, and I'd grow all my own fresh produce. I'd can and pickle and freeze every bit I could, and I'd feed my guests homegrown food."

"Sounds nice," Clarisse said, nodding.

"And I'd make homemade candy, too. I'd make chocolate truffles that I'd never sell commercially, but I'd make little baskets of candy and chocolate for every holiday. Like for Thanksgiving, I'd make maple brittle and hazelnut truffles, and for Christmas I'd make peppermint—" She stopped and laughed. "But who has that kind of time?"

"It's still nice to dream," her aunt said. "And don't give up on that. You might do it yet."

"My brothers would only sneak in and take it." The smiled slipped, and Lily sighed, a mental image of all that hard work being gobbled up by greedy mouths. "They're out of control."

Clarisse nodded. "We all know it."

And that seemed to be how every dream of hers faded—with the realization that her brothers would ruin it if she let them close enough. Except for her business—she'd started that up anyway, and she was determined to find a way to make this work. She was constantly protecting the boys, or protecting everything else from them.

"But while we're talking about crazy, impossible dreams," Lily added quietly, rubbing gentle circles on the baby's back, "I'd keep Emily."

"You would?" Clarisse stopped chopping and came around the counter. "Are you serious about that?"

"Like I said, crazy and impossible," Lily said quickly. "But I'd love to raise a little girl of my own."

"And you can," Clarisse said. "You'll get married and have kids of your own someday."

Kids of her own. She'd always wanted a family—even with her exasperation with her brothers. She leaned her cheek gently against that downy head, and she realized it wasn't just "a baby" that she wanted, it was this baby. And that was a dangerous thing to even admit to, because it would only make it harder when her time with Emily was up.

"It doesn't matter," Lily said. "I have four little brothers and a business to run. I've got to keep my feet on the ground, especially with Bryce around. I don't know what I'm going to do—the visiting officers are my bread and butter."

Clarisse was silent for a moment, and then she put a hand on Lily's. "You are too young to stop dreaming, dear. They won't be boys forever. They'll grow up eventually, and you'll be mad as a hornet if you put off your dreams for that ungrateful lot."

Outside, the men loaded the steaks onto a plate, and their footsteps clomped along the deck as they got to the screen door. The aroma of barbecue-charred meat wafted through the kitchen as they came in. Aaron cast Clarisse a boyish grin, and her aunt blushed. Whether Aaron was a con man or not, one thing was certain—her aunt was in love.

Bryce brushed past Lily to put the plate of steaks on the table. His hand skimmed along her back as he edged by.

"Excuse me," he said, his voice low. He glanced

back at her after he'd passed, and her heart gave a squeeze.

Feet on the ground, Lily, she reminded herself. Her aunt might believe in hopes and dreams, but Lily was a little more pragmatic. Distraction wasn't even an option.

Chapter Five

As they drove back home later that evening, Bryce breathed in the scent of fresh grass from the open windows. The moon was high and full, spilling silvery light over the fields they passed, the shadowy shapes of cows rising like mounds in the grass. A few clouds stretched across the sky—a soothing night drive.

It had been an interesting evening, and seeing Lily with her relatives had been eye-opening. Normally, if he was meeting a woman's family, there would be an added pressure on him to fit in or impress them, but with Lily, since their association was purely professional—whether her aunt believed that or not—he had the pleasure of simply observing.

Lily and her aunt seemed especially close, and Lily relaxed in a different way when they talked. She trusted Clarisse, that much was clear, but Lily's distrust of Aaron was equally obvious. If Aaron noticed, he didn't let on. They slowed to a stop for an intersection, and he glanced over at Lily. If he weren't here being disciplined, he'd ask her out…but not like this.

"So what did Aaron say about my aunt?" Lily asked, breaking the easy silence.

When Bryce and Aaron had stood outside with the barbecue, Aaron had talked more openly than when they were around the women. Mostly, he'd told Bryce that Clarisse was protective of Lily, and by extension, so was he. They didn't want to see Lily get hurt—or at least that was the image Aaron had adopted. After Bryce went through the motions of reassuring him that he wasn't involved with Lily in any way, Aaron had relaxed somewhat and talked about his relationship with Clarisse.

"He said he'd met your aunt in a chat room on a Christian dating site, and he hadn't realized her age at first. But the more he got to know her, the more he knew he was falling for her. So when they did discover the age difference, they had to have a serious talk about it."

Lily made a turn onto a paved road, her gaze flickering toward him only for a moment. "So he admitted that the age difference was…odd."

"Not really," he said. "He did say that they understand each other in a way that no one else seems to. He says she can really make him laugh."

Lily was silent.

"Sounded like love to me," he said quietly.

Bryce had dated a few women over the years, and he'd gotten serious with one of them—Kelly. She had been a volunteer at the station, working with women caught up in domestic abuse. They'd dated for a couple of years. She'd known from the beginning that he didn't want kids, and he'd thought that she was okay with that. And then one Christmas he'd bought her an engagement ring. She'd been hinting about wanting to get married, and when she opened the tiny box that Christmas Eve, her eyes lit up, and then she froze.

"Before I say yes," she'd said softly, "I just need to know that you're open to having kids one day."

That was when it crumbled. They broke up that Christmas, and they'd gone their separate ways to nurse their broken hearts. But before it all ended, he'd experienced what it felt like to be in love. He also knew what it felt like to let a woman down.

So while Bryce could be sympathetic to someone being in love, he hadn't exactly lost his cynicism. Feelings only took a couple so far.

"So you're done investigating?" she asked.

Bryce laughed softly. "Didn't say that. I just said that it sounded like love, but if he is a con man, he'd know how to fake that."

From the backseat, the baby started to cry, and Lily immediately tensed. She glanced in the rearview mirror, then tried to look into the backseat, but wasn't able to. Emily's thin wail filled the car.

Bryce stretched to get a better look at the baby. Her little eyes were scrunched up and her bottom lip quivered in despair. Obviously, he couldn't just pick her up, so he looked around for an alternative. Her pacifier lay on the seat beside her, and he gave it a quick wipe on his sleeve and popped it into her mouth.

The result was silence, and he felt a wave of victory.

"What did you do?" Lily asked.

"Pacifier." He glanced back at the baby again, and her eyes were shining in the darkness, the pacifier bobbing up and down in a soft staccato.

"You're better at this than you admit," she said. "You

said you weren't good with kids, but you seem to have a special touch with Emily."

Kelly had thought the same thing, and it was better to shut this down than to let Lily keep thinking something that Bryce knew was impossible. He was the spitting image of his father in more ways than he was proud of, and while he might be able to handle some basic child-related duties from time to time, he wasn't good *for* kids.

"You wouldn't say that if you saw me in my natural habitat." He meant to sound more joking than it came out, but it was hard to jest about the flat truth. He didn't know how to relate to kids, and he already knew that kind of ability couldn't be learned.

"How so?"

Here it was—the inevitable conversation that ended whatever it was that ever started with a woman. Kelly had held out after this conversation, but she'd been wrong to do that. He'd told her the truth, and no amount of wishing or hoping could change it. He'd rather let a woman down earlier than later, when there was less to lose. And while he knew that nothing had started with Lily, he still found himself wary in a way he probably didn't have a right to.

"I'm a nice guy," he said. "I'm a good guy. I believe in telling the truth and making the world a safer place for those kids. But I'm not much of a dad."

"If you don't have kids, you aren't a dad at all," she said, frowning slightly. "I think that's the sort of role you grow into."

Some men didn't grow into the role. His father certainly hadn't, and apparently his grandfather hadn't been much better—the Camden men with their dark hair and blue eyes, and superhuman ability to disappoint.

"Maybe with most guys," he agreed, "but I'm not most guys. And I've got a pretty good idea of how I'd turn out in the end because I'm exactly like my dad."

Everyone said it. From teachers to extended family, everyone commented on how much he was like his father. He looked like his dad, he walked like his dad, he even had his father's sense of humor. In fact, he'd probably have gotten along with his father pretty well in adulthood if the man had stuck around and actually parented, but he hadn't, and that was something else he shared with his father: some kids liked him, but he didn't feel comfortable around them. Kids were complicated little creatures, and he didn't know how to give them the things they needed. He was better off sticking to his strengths and letting someone else nurture the next generation.

"You said he left when you were young," Lily said.

He sighed. She wasn't letting this go, apparently. If she wanted to talk, he didn't mind. Besides, this was one less thing he'd have to write in that notebook.

"Yeah. I did see him from time to time, and one night after I got myself into some trouble, my dad did some actual parenting and sat me down for a talk." He could still see his father in his mind's eye. He'd been tall and good-looking—wearing a sports jersey and jeans—and Bryce had been filled with conflicted emotions at the sight of him. Part of him resented his dad for every single disappointment in his childhood, and another part of him missed him so much it hurt.

"We didn't see each other often, and so I figured I'd get some answers while I could," he went on. "I asked why he left, why he didn't want anything to do with me anymore, and he said that he just didn't know how to do the family thing. He said he knew what it looked like, and he knew how to act the part, but a guy could only fake it for so long."

Like a ticking time bomb for heartbreak. So far, Lily hadn't treated him like something about to go off, but maybe she'd be wise to consider it. The fact that his father had feigned being a father to his son had been a painful realization. Bryce had craved more from his dad, hoped for some untapped well of relationship. There hadn't been one.

"That's awful." Lily looked over at him in sympathy. "Really awful. Boys need their dads."

Her warmth helped, somehow. At least she understood the pain. This wasn't something he talked about often, and maybe it was the transitory nature of this relationship that made him feel more comfortable opening up to her. They were silent for a moment, and Lily seemed to be mulling over the things he'd just said. Finally, she shot him a quizzical look.

"What was he talking about, pretending?" she asked. "That sounds like a cop-out to me."

Bryce chuckled. He liked her—she didn't accept halfway answers, even on his behalf. How to explain it all...

"My dad just wasn't cut out for fatherhood," he said. "I made my peace with that. And he did love me—he still does, for that matter." His father had called the chief on his behalf, after all. If that wasn't love, he didn't know what was. "But he couldn't give me the relationship I needed. I think there are an awful lot of men out there like that. They mean well, and they do try to be better than they are, but at the end of the day, they're lousy fathers. They say you should fake it till you make it…but what if you never make it?"

He couldn't imagine looking into his own son's face and seeing that disappointment. Whenever he dealt with kids out in the field, he passed them off to another officer as quickly as possible. He used to try, but he'd never seemed to connect with them like the other officers could. They always needed something that he didn't know how to provide—comfort, reassurance, answers—and he'd stopped fighting that. They needed someone who wouldn't be muddling through. Those kids deserved better than he could give.

"It doesn't mean you have to end up like him," Lily countered.

"I already am."

He cleared his throat and looked out the window. There was no un-ringing that bell—he was a Camden man, and some things came as part of that genetic package.

"So you don't want kids." Her tone had changed slightly, and when he looked over at her, her gaze was riveted to the road. They were nearing town now, and she slowed down and signaled a turn.

"No," he admitted quietly. "I don't."

But that didn't mean that he'd lost hope in his future. Maybe he'd never be a father, and maybe that meant he wouldn't be a husband, either, but he knew for sure that God was leading in his life.

But seeing Lily with the baby, her life here in Comfort Creek and the depth of possibility in those clear blue eyes of hers…it made his reality a little harder to bear.

* * *

A few minutes later, Lily turned into the gravel drive that led up to her house. The windows were dark, but a porch light glowed warm and soft, illuminating two rocking chairs and the circular table between them. It was a perfect spot to sit on a summer night—something she'd put thought into. This was for her guests, a relaxing place to enjoy a piece of pie and some iced tea, and on the rare evenings—at least she hoped they'd be rare—that she didn't have guests, she'd make use of it herself. Now it looked lonely, somehow.

Her porch. Her house. Her guests. It still felt crazy and exciting to be thinking in terms of ownership. Getting here had been a gift from above, and she'd never lost her gratefulness.

It feels like home.

She'd loved this house for as long as she could remember. For years, it was owned by a quiet old couple. When they passed away and the house was up for sale, Lily bought it. This house was perfect—and yet she still felt a little ache of something missing. She'd fought so long and hard to get something of her own, prayed endlessly for just one chance to make something of herself, that now that she was finally here it felt wrong to admit that it wasn't enough. God had blessed her with so much, but there was still a part of her heart that longed for one more blessing to make this home perfect—a family to share it with. Guests would fill the house with life, but a family would make it a home.

An image of her brothers shot into her mind. Lily had family—all sorts of it—clambering around the edges and pushing to get in. So family in the broader sense wasn't her answer, either.

Lily parked the car and turned around to look at Emily, now fast asleep again.

"You know, I wasn't sure I wanted kids, either," she said after a moment. "I got my fill of wrangling youngsters with my brothers, so when I imagined the life I wanted, I never included kids in the fantasy."

She couldn't really blame Bryce for his choice. Like he said, there were probably a good number of men who should have made a similar decision. She pulled a hand through her hair, tugging it away from her forehead.

"Are you saying you'd be happy without kids?" Bryce's tone was cautious, and when she looked over at him, he met her gaze. Was he asking this for personal reasons? If he'd asked her a couple of years ago, she might have said yes, but that answer would have been both premature and naive.

"No." She shrugged. "I always knew I wanted some time to myself, a chance to chase my own dreams and start my own life, so kids weren't part of those daydreams, but I don't think I ever imagined I wouldn't have children ever. I do want kids, I just hadn't thought of having them this early. Does that make sense?"

Bryce nodded. "Yeah."

And then there was little Emily…a baby she knew she couldn't keep, but who had awoken something inside her that she hadn't expected to feel.

"It's always been a bit of a problem for me," Bryce said, and she heard a note of regret in his voice that caught at her heart. "It's a deal breaker for women. Most women, at least. The ones I end up being attracted to."

Did that include her? She quickly pushed the thought back. It shouldn't matter, but somehow it did.

"I almost got married two years ago," he went on quietly.

"What happened?" she asked.

"I didn't want kids." He looked over at her and met her gaze. "I think she thought she'd change my mind, and I'd been dumb enough to think that maybe I'd be enough for her."

"But you weren't."

"No, I wasn't." He pulled in a deep breath, then sighed. "But that's reality. That's life. I can't ask a woman to give up on having children, grandchildren, all of that."

Bryce had fallen in love with someone, and Lily found herself a little envious of that woman. She'd been able to look into his face and see that depth of feeling... If things were different, she might have been tempted, too.

"Where is she now?" Lily asked.

"We lost touch. It was a mutual breakup. We both cared for each other, but it obviously wasn't going to work."

She could sense deeper heartbreak beneath the words, but he didn't look willing to go further.

"She broke your heart," Lily said.

Bryce smiled sadly. "Yeah, she did. So what about you? Who broke yours?"

She was surprised at that question, because she'd never hinted that she harbored any heartbreak.

"What makes you think anyone did?" she asked.

"I'm a cop," he said. "I know how to read people, and you're too cautious to have gotten away unscathed."

He was right, of course, and she hadn't thought about Austin for quite some time.

"All right. His name was Austin, and he was my

high school boyfriend. He left for college, and he swore that we'd survive the long-distance relationship."

And she'd believed him when he said that she was the only one he could possibly love. It seemed so naive now.

"Let me guess." A smile flickered at the corners of his lips. "You had plans to go see him, or he had plans to come see you, and instead, you got an email saying that he'd met someone else and maybe you shouldn't meet up after all."

"A phone call, actually," she said. "But yes. How did you know?"

"Tale as old as time." His expression softened. "If it counts for anything, he was an idiot to have left you to begin with."

She smiled and looked back out the window toward the house. Maybe he hadn't been such an idiot after all. Austin wouldn't have wanted to do this, and he wouldn't have fit into her dreams, either. He wanted city and bustle, and she wanted Comfort Creek. This town was where her family was, where her heart was. She had no desire to go to the big city, and Austin had no desire to stay put. There was no middle ground, and if there was one thing she'd learned from that experience it was to keep her feet planted. Some people had the luxury of having their heads in the clouds, but she didn't. If she was going to make anything of her life, she'd have to stay realistic.

"I think that God had a hand in it," she said after a moment. "Austin married that someone else, after all."

"Ouch." Bryce winced. "Sorry."

"No, it's fine," she said with a shake of her head. "I mean, it was a blow to my ego, but I'm not so self-centered that I think that God can't be working out someone else's love story, too. Austin and I wanted different things. If we'd stubbornly stuck together in spite of that, it wouldn't have been a happily-ever-after."

Bryce nodded. "I could see that."

"Besides—" She nodded toward the house. "This is what I want."

She wished she felt as confident as she sounded. She did want this bed-and-breakfast, but there was still that nagging feeling that something was missing. From the backseat, Emily made some sucking sounds on her pacifier, and Lily wished that her heart didn't swell every time she heard those soft noises from the infant.

"I'd better get inside," Lily said. "Thank you for coming tonight. I appreciate it."

"No problem." His voice was a quiet rumble.

She glanced over to where he sat, and those blue eyes were fixed on her. He was a good-looking man, and being in these close quarters only served to remind her how handsome he was, and that wasn't helping matters right now.

She turned away to open the door when his voice stopped her.

"But would you have married him?"

"Austin?" she asked with a frown.

"Yeah. I mean, he broke your heart and moved on, but if he hadn't —if he'd stayed faithful—would you have married him?"

It hardly seemed like a fair question, since she'd never had the chance to choose. But if he'd been faithful to her and returned her love… She could see now that marrying him would have meant compromising on everything that mattered most to her, but she wouldn't have seen that before.

"Probably," she said with a sigh.

And she'd have stayed married, too, because she was a woman who believed in those vows. Would a loving husband and a couple of kids of her own have been enough? Would she have been satisfied making a home in Denver with Austin?

She'd miss out on all of her brothers' antics, all of their trouble, all of the stress that came with those four boys, and she'd be too far away to do anything for them. Somehow, she just couldn't erase her brothers from the equation, either.

She got out of the car, then got the baby from the backseat. When she straightened again, she caught Bryce watching her.

"You really would have married him when it came right down to it?" Bryce asked.

Why did that seem to matter to him so much? "Wouldn't you have married your girlfriend?"

"And then spent the next decade fighting over whether or not to have kids," he quipped.

"Well, we're older now," she said. "Hopefully a little wiser, too."

They walked together toward the front door, and Lily pulled out her keys. They stood shoulder to shoulder, and she felt her heart swelling again in spite of herself. Feeling anything for Bryce was a bad idea...

"Let me give you a hand," he said, and his warm fingers brushed hers as he took the car seat from her grasp.

"Thanks, I—" She turned toward him, and found his face hovering just above hers. They were still, standing there on the porch, Bryce's biceps flexed under the weight of the car seat. He didn't move, though, and when his glittering eyes met hers, she felt her breath catch in her throat. She dragged her gaze down and turned back to the key in the lock.

This all felt a little too domestic for her comfort. It was too cozy, and she was liking it too much. Bryce was warm, gentle, open... And this was a new experience for her, to have a tiny baby in her care and a strong man beside her, lending a hand and sparking feelings inside her that didn't belong there. She was used to shouldering things alone, and she'd best remember it, because her life wasn't about to get any easier. He was her temporary guest, and if he was the reason her brothers ended up with criminal records before she could straighten them out, she wasn't sure she'd forgive herself.

"If you're interested in a snack before bed, I have banana bread in the fridge," Lily said as she turned the key in the lock and pushed open the front door. "I also have skim milk and whole milk to wash it down. If you like two percent—" she flipped on the light in the hallway "—I guess you'll just have to mix them."

Lily locked the door behind them with a *click* and stepped away from him. "Thanks," Bryce said, and she didn't miss the quizzical look he cast her. He didn't understand her sudden professional rigidity, she could tell, but he'd just have to live with a little mystery, because she wasn't going to explain. He might not have felt anything out there, but she had. She took the car seat back.

"Clean towels are on the counter in the bathroom, and breakfast will ready at seven thirty. Unless you'd like to get to the station earlier, in which case I can be flexible."

"Lily." His tone hadn't changed from earlier, still low and warm. "Are you okay?"

"Professional boundaries," she said. "I'm giving them another try."

"Okay." He nodded, and an amused smile flickered across his face. "Well then, thank you for a lovely evening, and I won't be late for breakfast."

What she needed to do was to get back to her cottage and have some silence and solitude, and hopefully get her emotions back into order.

"Good night," she said, and she turned her steps toward the back door. She looked down at the sleeping face of little Emily, and sent up a prayer:

Lord, help me to guard my heart.

Chapter Six

Comfort Creek felt lonelier without Lily's friendliness in it. He did his patrol, dealing with a neighborly dispute over lawn fertilizer—one neighbor used it, the other neighbor didn't want "poison" to waft onto her organic vegetables.

The sorts of silly issues that nearly brought people to blows astounded to him. Not that he could be self-righteous when it came to fighting, he realized bitterly. And it wasn't just this situation with Leroy, either. He was his father's son, and his dad had been disciplined for excessive use of force twice—the two times he was caught. There had probably been other infractions like that, but he hadn't been reported.

Bryce was embarrassed about his father's track record, but he also understood it, too. No one knew what it was like to walk into a bar brawl with nothing but a billy club and bulletproof vest—that he intended to use, at least. A gun was a very last resort. A cop was a target, and any drunk biker that came at him wasn't playing by the same rules. No one called him "sir." No one politely ordered him to back down. No one was angling to subdue him without using any more force than necessary. They wanted to beat him to a pulp, get a knife under the vest or pull a gun. And he was supposed to face that with calm and a determination to respect the perpetrator's dignity? No one understood just how hard this job was, except someone who did it—like his father.

So Bryce could actually sympathize with his father on that point—not that he excused it. The times his father was brought up on charges for excessive force had been when he'd gotten a kick in after the perp was already subdued. That kind of thing was tempting when the perp had bitten you through your uniform and left bloody teeth marks on your arm, or had come at you with a dirty needle—the kind of needle that could give you life-altering diseases with just one jab. It was easy to take that personally, but he struggled to keep a professional outlook. Excessive force wasn't okay, no matter how angry he got.

So far—on the job, at least—Bryce had walked that line, and he hadn't crossed it. That was God's intervention, because if he hadn't been able to walk into bar brawls knowing that God was at his side, listening to that whisper in his heart, he knew he'd have gone the way of his father. It was the path of least resistance. God's way used a whole lot more self-control.

He sighed, raking a hand through his hair as he eased to a stop at an intersection. This town was giving him more time to think than he liked. It was just him and that ridiculous minivan, cruising down these boring streets. Four stoplights, two entrances to the highway, and a whole lot of nothing in between. Welcome to Comfort Creek.

A woman glanced at the van and stepped out to cross the road. She looked familiar—so familiar that it gave him a jolt—but upon closer inspection, she wasn't who he thought she was. Just another resident of this town...

His heart hammered in his throat, and he heaved a sigh. She looked a lot like a girl he'd known in high school. No one special to him. In fact, she'd been a year younger and had attended a party that he'd dropped in on. He'd been in a lot of trouble back then, making stupid choices, going to parties, drinking. She'd been young and defiant, and one of the older guys had zeroed in on her.

The woman finished crossing the road and continued down the street without a backward glance, but the memories she'd sparked were still close to the surface. He didn't like to think about that night—the night a girl was nearly assaulted and he'd stepped in to stop it. Except he hadn't been a cop then; he'd been a seventeen-year-old kid. And he hadn't had any training on walking that line...

Bryce eased the vehicle forward and crawled down the street toward the downtown core once more. He scanned the shade-dappled yards that he passed. Perfect peace and quiet. There weren't even any kids on this street...a couple of lazy dogs in the shade that looked up at him but didn't even bother to bark, the ripple of an American flag from a staff in a front yard.

He hoped the girl had gone on to live a life like this one, in a town quiet and tranquil. It would make him feel better to know that, because he'd done it for her—a girl he barely knew. The boy who hadn't been able to take no for an answer had spent a couple of days in the hospital with three broken ribs and a dislocated jaw, and Bryce had been picked up by the cops for assault. He could still remember the blood on his knuckles.

That was one night his father decided to do a bit of parenting and sat him down for a talk. His dad managed to get the charges dropped—had a heart-to-heart with the father of the guy Bryce had pummeled—and then sat down with Bryce for the conversation that would forever alter the trajectory of his life.

"Here's the thing, Bryce," his dad said seriously. "You're just like me, so I get it. There's always a reason. But you've got to be careful. I got you off this time, but next time, I might not be able to, and that would have been criminal charges. You're old enough that they could have bumped it to adult court."

"But he was about to—"

"I don't care." His father heaved a sigh. "Look—I got you off. Let's just let this go."

And that was when Bryce decided to ask a few questions of his own about why his dad had been absent for so long. His father told him that he wasn't father material, and that there was no helping it. But there was more to the conversation than Bryce had told Lily...

"Bryce, you're old enough to understand this now," his father had told him. "You're exactly like me, so you'd better take this seriously. You have my temper. You have my weaknesses. So be careful."

"I'm not like you," Bryce had snapped. "You left. I've taken care of Mom myself."

"Your mom kicked me out."

Bryce could still remember listening to his own heartbeat inside his head as those words sank in. "That's not true."

But all of his mother's words came flooding back… all of the times she'd shouted at him in sheer frustration: *You're just like your father!*

He'd assumed it was because she was afraid that he'd leave, too, that he'd abandon her. But maybe it was deeper than that…maybe he was just like his dad, and she could see the writing on the wall. Maybe it took all the self-control she had to not kick him out, too. Maybe she wasn't hoping he'd stay.

That day had changed everything for Bryce. That was the day he'd grown up.

Bryce looked down at his knuckles on the steering wheel and sighed. These hands were capable of evil, and he hated that. He hated that when he was faced with a split-second decision, he'd landed on the side of violence. He'd told himself that he'd never do that again—this was a onetime mistake. But when nagged and needled by Leroy, he'd snapped. It wasn't who he wanted to be, but it did show him who he was: his father's son.

He took a left onto Main Street, easing past the now-familiar stores. The silver lining to the whole debacle had been that a teenage girl had gone home safe—shaken and scared, but safe. He'd been protecting her, but the Camden in him had been too strong.

Years later, Bryce had found some solidarity with the apostle Paul. Some men weren't meant for family life, and Paul made that okay. Bryce had hoped to get married one day, but what woman wanted a broken cop who wouldn't have kids? He thought Kelly might be his saving grace, but when it came down to the line, she'd wisely walked away. And he hadn't blamed her.

Bryce glanced at his watch. His shift was almost

over. He'd told Lily that he'd be back for dinner, but he wasn't sure he wanted to face her right now. Maybe it was better to grab a burger and keep his distance. But if he wasn't going to eat the dinner Lily was preparing, he'd better at least give her some warning. Plus there was a minivan backseat filled with zucchini from an old woman's front garden. He pulled to the side of the road in front of the hardware store and dialed his cell phone.

"Hello?" Lily sounded breathless, and in the background, Emily's cry reverberated.

"Hi, it's Bryce." He pulled the phone away from his ear as Emily's cry got louder. "Everything okay?"

"Uh—" There was a clatter, a thump, Lily's voice crooning to the baby, and then she said, "Sorry, dropped the phone. How are you?"

"Better than you, by the sounds of it," he quipped. "What's going on over there?"

"I need a hand with something, if it's not too much trouble."

"Sure," he said. "What do you need?"

"Another pacifier. I dropped Emily's in the garbage disposal by accident, and she is just furious about it. Can you pick one up for me and bring it by?"

He could hear the wince in her voice, and Emily's cry hadn't lessened in the least. He had a feeling she'd forgotten about dinner, which was just as well. But he couldn't leave her a lurch like that.

"No problem. I'll be there in a few minutes." He had to raise his voice for Lily to hear him, and a couple coming out of the hardware store looked over at him in curiosity.

"Wait, what did you call about?" she asked.

He'd called to bail out on dinner, to excuse himself and frankly, just to hear her voice.

"It's nothing. I'll see you soon."

He hung up his phone and nodded to the couple, who were still watching him. He pulled a U-turn, then signaled a turn south on Sycamore Drive. That was where the Comfort Creek Drug Mart was located, and it was his best guess as to where he'd find baby paraphernalia.

How hard could it be to buy a pacifier?

Lily deposited the phone on the kitchen counter. Reinforcements would be here soon... Was she really able to handle a baby on her own? She'd been toying with the thought of keeping Emily, but she couldn't help but wonder if she was being naive.

Emily was propped up on Lily's shoulder, her crying less insistent now, and it looked like the infant might have actually cried herself out.

"It's not so terrible, sweetheart," she said softly, patting Emily's back. "I'm getting you a new one, I promise."

And yet she had to wonder how much babies this tiny understood about the world around them. Did she remember her mother still in some part of her little heart? Was she confused about the changes, the different people holding her and feeding her? Did it ever get to be just too much to handle so that she cried and cried? It wouldn't be the last time in Emily's life that she felt like she couldn't handle any more—that was life—but if she could be sheltered from the brunt of it...

Father, protect this little girl, she prayed silently as she rocked the baby back and forth, her whimpers slowly subsiding. *Comfort her where I can't...*

Emily needed a mother—a family. She needed someone who would care for her for the rest of her life, who be committed to her welfare. She didn't need the child welfare system, she needed an honest-to-goodness family, and there was only one whom Lily trusted to provide that.

When Lily was a little girl before her father passed away, her mother used to sit on the side of her bed and sing her a good-night song every night. It was always the same song, just a simple Sunday school tune, but it had comforted Lily like nothing else. When she got older, she still sang that song to herself because it reminded her of simpler times, and it pointed her to the father who would never die on her or leave her scrambling to deal with life without Him.

So as she rocked Emily, Lily hummed that tune, and the longer she hummed, the calmer Emily became until those teary eyes began to droop, wet lashes brushing against plump cheeks.

"I love you, little one," Lily whispered, and her heart ached with the weight of that love. Grief was the price one paid for having loved, and she would pay dearly for having fallen for this little girl, because someone else would come and take her away and Lily would have to let go.

Footsteps clunked up the outside steps, and then the front door opened, and she glanced up to see Bryce look inside uncertainly.

"Is she sleeping?" he asked quietly.

"Just dropped off." She gestured him to come in by tipping her head to the side. "But the minute she wakes up, I'm going to need that pacifier, so I really appreciate this."

Bryce stepped inside, a plastic bag in one hand, and it looked a little full for the item she'd requested. He held up the bag with a small smile.

"I got every single kind they had."

Lily laughed softly. "How many kinds *did* they have?"

"Eight."

He headed down the hall toward the kitchen, and she followed behind him. Emily heaved a shaky sigh in her sleep as if her sadness had followed her. If a pacifier would bring this baby comfort, then Emily would have one. By the looks of it, she'd have eight.

Bryce dumped the pacifiers out onto the kitchen table, and she chuckled as she saw the selection. There were some for newborns, for toddlers, and even a package of bottle nipples.

"Those aren't pacifiers," she said with a soft laugh.

"Don't care," he said. "I got everything that even looked like one."

This was the first time she'd seen Bryce look out of his element. From the moment she'd set eyes on him, he always seemed so cool and collected, but standing there with an empty plastic bag in one hand and a selection of pacifiers and pacifier approximations in front of him on the kitchen table, he was endearingly awkward.

"That pink one—" she said, nodding toward one package. "That looks about right. We'll have to boil it. You had no idea what you were looking for, did you?" She chuckled.

"Not a clue. I'm just glad you didn't send me for something harder, like diapers or something." He spoke quietly so as not to disturb the baby.

"You're her hero," Lily said, looking down into Emily's sleeping face. "At least you will be once she wakes up. I wonder if I can get her into the bassinet."

It took a couple of tries, but Lily laid Emily in the bassinet at last and pulled the receiving blanket over her bare legs. She slowly straightened.

"There…" She crossed the room again and stood next to Bryce by the counter, her gaze moving out the kitchen window toward her cottage.

"You look tired," Bryce said.

"That was about two hours of solid crying," Lily said with a shake of her head. "Poor thing, but there was no way I was rooting a pacifier out of the garbage disposal."

"Good call."

When she looked up, she saw his blue eyes fixed on her in a way that made her feel warmer because of his presence. She'd missed him today—something she'd blamed on the fussy baby and Bryce's gifted touch with Emily—but if there was more to her feelings, she didn't want to explore them. Not with Bryce standing here and looking at her like that. She never seemed to think straight with him looking at her.

"So how was your day?" she asked.

"Oh, that's right." Bryce's arm was close to hers— so close that she could have leaned into him, but she didn't. "I bought a lot of zucchini."

She frowned. "Why?"

"Long story, but it ends with me personally owning more zucchini than I know what to do with. So I was wondering if you wanted them."

Lily shrugged. "Sure. I could make some deep-fried zucchini spears. Those tend to be a crowd-pleaser. And I'm sure my mom could find some use for them, too."

"Great." He gave a curt nod. "That takes care of that."

Yet despite their casual back-and-forth, they still stood inches away from each other. It was to stay quiet enough to let the baby sleep, she told herself, but that didn't explain the way her stomach flipped when he looked at her.

"So...do you want to tell me more about how exactly you came across this haul of zucchini?" she asked.

"I bought them from Beatrice Nubbles. She's on a fixed income and she can't enter her zucchini into the organic vegetable contest this year since hers aren't exactly organic anymore, and I got the feeling she needed the prize money."

So he'd bought Mrs. Nubbles's zucchini... It was a surprisingly sweet thing to do, and she found herself smiling up at him.

"You are a lot more sensitive than you let on, you know," she said.

"You think?" He raised an eyebrow and caught her eye with a teasing smile. "Because I'm really not. What you see is what you get. I'm a lout."

Why did he do that? It was more than deflecting a compliment; it was pushing away any good opinion anyone had of him. Did he not believe it of himself, or was he just trying to keep her at a distance? She was his hostess, and she needed to act like it. She straightened her spine and took a step away from Bryce. He seemed to notice her retreat, because his expression turned curious, but he didn't move. She was out of control again—she cast about for something to say that would bring things back to a professional standing.

"With the weekend approaching," she said, "I thought I should tell you that Sunday mornings I'm in church. But I can leave a cold breakfast in the fridge for you. I hope that isn't an inconvenience."

He shook his head. "I'll be fine. I'll probably be in church, too. I've got to bring my truck in for an oil change afterward, but I don't like missing the service."

"Would you like to come to our church?"

As soon as the words came out, she knew she'd crossed yet another line, and heat rose in her cheeks. Appropriate reserve would have been giving him the addresses of the three churches and allowing him the privacy to choose his own place of worship, yet here she was inviting him along. However, she'd also sent him shopping for pacifiers, so perhaps she'd already galloped so far over those lines that there was no return.

"I'd like that." His voice was deep and quiet.

The foot and a half between them felt like a gulf with those blue eyes and the direct stare. He was tall and strong, and he made her feel flustered. But this was her fault. She was the one who set the tone for her establishment, and she'd done a poor job of maintaining a proper decorum.

"Bryce, I want to apologize. I'm not being as professional as I should."

"This is a weird situation," he replied.

Was it? It felt that way, but when she examined the situation objectively, she couldn't really defend that.

"No, it isn't. I'm providing a service, and you are my guest. This shouldn't be complicated at all."

"And yet it is." His tone was quiet, and he almost sounded like he was talking to himself. But he was voicing the same thing that she was thinking—that while they had no good reason for this tension, it was still there.

"Look, extreme experiences change boundaries a bit. In my job, this happens a lot. When I have a partner on patrol, I end up a lot closer to that officer than I'd be to a regular coworker if I had a standard nine-to-five job. Extreme situations warp the boundaries a bit."

"But we aren't partners on patrol," she reminded him.

"No, but we are caring for a newborn."

Lily looked toward the bassinet and smiled sadly. "Yes, I suppose we are."

"And while I'd like to keep my emotional distance from Piglet, I'm not doing a really great job of that, either. So don't be too hard on yourself. You'd have been perfectly businesslike if there weren't a baby in the mix," he said.

Was that all this was—a reaction to having a newborn to care for? It would be a huge relief if this could all be so easily explained and filed away. Babies did change things... Her brothers had been the same.

"Is that what this is?" she asked.

"Let me put it this way," he said. "It's going to be really hard to say goodbye to that little girl when the time comes. I know what I have to do, but that doesn't make it any easier. So maybe you could just start those boundaries with the next guy."

Lily laughed softly. "Are we past the point of no return here?"

"I think so."

"I'd wanted to be different than this," she confessed. "In my head, I'm much more refined."

"I like you this way." His gaze warmed, and he cast her a smile.

He was so reassuring that she was inclined to believe him. He made her feel like the best version of herself when she was standing there in front of him, even if she questioned that version once she was safely by herself again.

Bryce pushed himself off the counter and glanced at his watch. "I guess I'd better get going."

"Dinner!" she exclaimed. As quickly as that, the moment was past, and real life rushed back into the room.

"It's okay," he said. "I was planning on getting a burger tonight anyway."

Was he? Or was he just being kind and letting her off the hook?

"Did you want to come along?" he asked.

"No." She shook her head quickly. "Thanks, though. I'll be fine."

She had cleaning to do, some cinnamon rolls to bake for tomorrow's breakfast. She also wanted to call her mom and brothers tonight. Her family needed her, too, and she'd been so wrapped up with her B and B that she was feeling guilty.

Bryce shot her a grin. "Okay. I'll see you later then."

She nodded, and he disappeared down the hallway. The front door opened and shut, and she was left alone in the kitchen thinking about the next time she'd see him. He'd said that if it weren't for Emily, she'd be perfectly businesslike, but she wasn't so sure about that. He was getting past all of her defenses and down to her heart.

Chapter Seven

Bryce's mother had raised him to go to church. While his father had never cared a whole lot whether he went to service or not, it was one thing his mother would not bend on in his boyhood years. He could still remember the verses she'd help him learn—stuck to the refrigerator with a magnet so that neither of them would forget their nightly ritual.

For God so loved the world that he gave his only son...

He'd learned a good portion of scripture because of the dedication of his mother and his Sunday school teachers. He'd learned right from wrong, and he'd accepted Jesus as his savior. And while that had given him an excellent foundation on which to build his life, it hadn't filled the hole left behind by his father. Not that the other officers in Fort Collins needed to know any of that. All they knew was that he was a Christian, and that a Christian cop was being disciplined for striking a fellow officer. He knew that God had forgiven him for this error in judgment, but he hadn't forgiven himself.

His fellow officers expected more of him. If they were telling inappropriate jokes, they toned it down when he came into earshot. They didn't take God's name in vain around him, and if they did, they apologized. It wasn't that he'd ever said anything to them, but the fact that he was a Christian meant something to them. But it meant something to him, too, and just because he'd messed up didn't mean he got to walk away from his spiritual touchstone.

Sunday morning, Bryce sat in the Hand of Comfort Christian Church—a play on words for the name of the town, if he'd ever heard one—with Lily beside him and the baby asleep on her lap. Lily was wearing that cherry dress she'd had on the first time he'd met her, and he found it oddly soothing. She looked peaceful, her gaze turned downward, her milky white skin glowing under the light of a stained glass window.

Sitting in church next to a beautiful woman who intrigued him in ways he'd never experienced before, looking down at the baby who had stolen his heart against his better judgment…it made him long for something down so deep that it felt like an ache. This was the sort of thing he should write in his little notebook—pretending this was his family, if only for a moment. He was allowing himself to go through the motions of starting something, even though he knew that Lily saw straight through him—but he wouldn't write anything in that notebook. Not today. He had the weekend off, so he figured it was only fair to take a vacation from writing in the notebook, too. Sunday could be a day of rest from self-recriminations, as well.

The offering plate had been passed, hymns had been sung, and the pastor had just stood up to preach. He was a large man with strong features and a humble tone. The pastor's wife seemed to be the obviously pregnant woman at the piano, because the pastor referred to her as "sweetheart," and it struck Bryce as rather touching.

"He's a new pastor here," Lily whispered, leaning closer. "He's a good preacher. I think you'll like him."

Bryce wondered what it would be like to belong in a place like Comfort Creek, to be a part of the story here. There were times when he was in Fort Collins that he'd fantasize about starting over in some little town somewhere. He'd open a business and reinvent himself…but some problems couldn't be escaped so easily—they followed a man around with the tenacity of friendly mutt—and he couldn't escape who he was.

Emily squirmed and let out a whimper. Lily pulled a bottle from her bag and popped it into her mouth. What was it about this particular baby's dedication to draining a bottle that softened him like this? He reached over and tweaked one of Emily's little socked feet. Her foot was so tiny, and when he let go, she thrust her foot out again toward him. She wanted his touch.

Bryce wrapped his hand gently around that tiny foot, and he felt tears mist his eyes as he turned his attention to the pastor's sermon. She drank her bottle like that—her foot in his hand, and he stroked her socked foot with his thumb, wondering if there would be the tiniest part of Emily that would remember him.

Was God testing him? Was there special spiritual value in a broken heart? He'd spent years trying to avoid this—getting attached and getting hurt—and here he was heart-deep with a baby girl he'd never see again once he left Comfort Creek.

The pastor was preaching on forgiveness—a topic he'd heard covered quite often in his home church in Fort Collins. But it wasn't the sermon topic that grabbed Bryce's interest, it was the illustration that he used.

"In 1988, a nineteen-year-old boy witnessed the murder of his elderly neighbor. Jacob Bernard was a promising student in his first year at college, home for Thanksgiving. He had just started dating a beautiful girl, and his future was bright. All he needed to do was to pretend he hadn't seen anything..."

The story went on, about how the boy had seen a mobster shoot this old lady as a message to someone the criminal was trying to manipulate, and if the boy had simply stayed mum, he'd have been able to go forward with his life. Instead, he decided to turn his back on his promising future, on the beautiful girl and on the loving home he'd been raised in, in order to testify in court against the mobster, and in return he was put into the witness protection program—a very lonely, quiet fresh start.

Bryce looked over at Lily, the idea so solidly in his mind that he couldn't believe he hadn't thought of it before. Lily looked up at him in surprise when she sensed his sudden tension.

"What?" she whispered.

"I have an idea..." He looked at his watch. It was half past eleven, and he knew exactly who to call. If Aaron Bay was in witness protection, then this would be beyond his pay grade. Thankfully he had a buddy in the FBI—very low level, but still, he could look into a few things for Bryce. "I'll be back in a few minutes."

Bryce stood and slipped past Lily's knees and into

the side aisle next to the stained glass window. The pastor went on with his sermon, and Bryce made his way out of the church as quietly as he could manage.

Once outside, on the sunny steps that led up to the doors, Bryce pulled out his phone and swiped through the phone book until he got to the number he was looking for. He touched the dial button, and as it rang, his gaze landed on two young men sitting on the curb across the street.

They had bottles covered in paper bags—so sneaky. No one would ever guess what was inside, he thought sarcastically. He rolled his eyes, then squinted to get a better look at them. They weren't Burke or Randy, which was a small relief. Lily had been through enough lately. They looked to be in their early teens—not very old, despite the practiced way they swigged at the bottles.

"That you, Bryce?" His friend picked up.

It didn't take long for Bryce to give the pertinent information and make his request. He'd return the favor sometime, if he was ever in the position.

After hanging up, he sauntered in the direction of the seated boys. They scooted behind a tree when they saw him coming, but they were clearly a little bit inebriated, because their movements were uncoordinated, and they guffawed a little too loudly, followed by a hissed "Shhhhhh!"

"Morning," Bryce said.

There was silence—as much silence as the boys could manage. It really consisted of some snuffled laughter.

"I see you," Bryce said. "And before you think of doing anything stupid, I'm a police officer."

The boys slowly emerged, minus the bottles, swaying slightly. They wore faded jeans and T-shirts with teenage bands on them. The closest boy pushed shaggy hair out of his face and peered at Bryce through bleary eyes. Now that he could get a good look at them, they looked almost identical, except one boy was slightly smaller.

"What're your names?" Bryce asked.

"Let's see your badge."

Bryce chuckled and pulled out his badge for their unfocused inspection. "Satisfied? Now what are your names?"

"Carson."

"Chris."

"Carson and Chris who?" Bryce asked, stifling a sigh. The boys obviously didn't want to say who they were, and they shuffled their feet, then froze when their gaze moved behind him.

"Ellison," a voice said behind him.

Bryce turned to see Lily standing there with the baby on one shoulder, the diaper bag on the other, and a look of blistering fury on her face.

When Bryce left the pew, Emily had started to fuss, and Lily had been forced to come outside to soothe the baby so that they wouldn't interrupt the service. Having done so, she immediately spotted and recognized her brothers. Carson and Chris were the babies of the family—less than a year old when Lily's father passed away. Chasing after rambunctious twins had kept everyone busy, especially Lily when the life insurance ran out and her mother had to go back to work in order to support them.

And there they stood, eyes bloodshot and booze bottles barely hidden in the grass. Her stomach dropped. She'd known that Randy and Burke had started to drink, but not the Little Ones.

"More brothers?" Bryce asked wryly.

It was even worse that this was in front of Bryce. He was a cop—would he report them to social services? And were they really this far into trouble that she was afraid for a law enforcement officer to see the reality of their family?

"The twins," she replied, anger welling up past the fear. "Twins who know better than this. Where did you get those bottles?"

"Burke."

"He gave it to you?" She was already planning some consequences for every single last one of them. It mostly consisted of jobs around the house, but given time she could come up with something more creative.

Chris looked away, and Carson's gaze dropped to the grass.

"Answer me." The baby started to whimper at Lily's tone, and Lily looked down at her big brown eyes. Emily didn't know what was going on but sensed everyone was upset. Lily sighed and gently jiggled the baby in her arms.

"I took it. He doesn't know," Carson said quietly.

That still didn't erase the fact that all four of her brothers were drinking, and obviously trying to get her attention with it, if they were doing it in front of the church. They needed her—but she didn't know what to give anymore. They were looking to her to fix something that she didn't know how to fix. She'd never felt more helpless in her life.

"You do realize that underage drinking and drinking in public are both illegal," Bryce said. The boys' eyes whipped toward Lily, their expression changing from sullen teenager to panicked child. They were scared now—as they should be. So was she.

"Tell him we're sorry," Chris said earnestly.

"Tell him we won't do it again," Carson added.

And there they were, looking to her to make it better, to take care of everything for them. At thirteen, they were barely more than children, and every time she looked at them, she remembered them as toddlers, standing there with sagging diapers and round eyes. They'd called her "Lily-please" for years.

"If you're grown up enough to break the law, then you're grown up enough to talk to me directly," Bryce said, crossing his arms over his chest.

The rage slipped out of her, and it was replaced by a clench of fear as the two boys looked up at the cop. *Lily-please, open this. Lily-please, get me the cereal. Lily-please, make me a snack...* When they did something stupid, she always reacted with anger first, but that was only because it was easier to be angry than to be so deeply sad and scared at the same time. And she *was* scared.

"Get in the car," she said quietly.

The boys trudged toward her familiar vehicle, out of earshot. They leaned back against the car without getting in, eyeing her with a mixture of uncertainty and defiance. Why couldn't teenagers be easier? They wanted her help, and yet they still wanted to stand right on the edge. She turned toward Bryce.

"Are you going to press charges?" she asked, trying to suppress the quiver in her voice.

"Do you want me to?" His tone was professional, and he fixed her with a direct stare. He wasn't feeling sorry for them like she was. The rest of the world didn't see little boys when they looked at Chris and Carson.

"No," she said softly. "Please, don't. I know this looks bad—you've seen the worst of us. But I'll take them home and sit them all down together for a long talk. Punishing can only take us so far, and my mom and I need a better plan…and more time."

"Okay."

"So…" She glanced toward them. "You'll let them off the hook this time?"

"Once." He crossed his arms over his chest. "And I'm serious about that, Lily. I catch them drinking again and I take them in."

It was fair, and she nodded quickly. "Got it. I'll make sure they understand that."

"But first, before you go—" his expression softened "—are you okay?"

Was she? She wasn't even sure. She was upset, out of her depth, scared for her brothers and unsure if she could even do anything about their troublesome ways. She wasn't okay—not in this respect at least—and she hadn't been for some time.

"I don't know what to do," she admitted, tears rising in her eyes.

"There are social service programs to help parents with out-of-control kids," he said. "They're good— they have no interest in taking kids away. They want to give families some tools to help get kids back on the straight and narrow."

"Social services," she whispered. She'd spent her entire childhood taking care of her brothers in order

to avoid social services being called into their home—
and they'd only missed it by a hair sometimes. Now
she was supposed to welcome them in with open arms?

"I'd hate that." She smiled wanly.

"It's an option," he said. "I'm just putting it out
there."

Professional intervention—it felt like failure to her.
When they had a home filled with love and the best
of intentions, they shouldn't need a government coun-
selor to step in.

"I'll take them home to my mom and we'll have a
family talk," she repeated. It was all she had, but it was
a start, and if they could find a way to pull together,
maybe she could figure out how to address this. And
if that didn't work, maybe they'd all have to suck up
their pride and ask for help.

"Why don't I take Emily back to the house?" Bryce
suggested. "Then you can take care of things with your
brothers."

"Will you be okay with that?" she asked, frowning. He'd made it pretty clear that he and babies didn't
mix, but all the same, she knew that Emily would be
perfectly safe with him.

"I'll figure it out," he said.

A flood of relief rushed over her. He was helping
more than he probably even realized. She'd been so
busy with the bed-and-breakfast, and now busy with
the baby, and perhaps what her brothers needed most
was some of her undivided attention. *Lily-please...*

All she'd wanted was a chance to focus on her own
life, but her brothers were a part of that life, and the
freedom she'd longed for seemed even further out of
reach. The other girls her age got to leave town, go

to college. They got to make their own mistakes, but Lily didn't have the luxury. There were no road trips with friends, or scmesters spent away from home. Just this—Comfort Creek and her family.

"Thank you, Bryce." She swallowed the lump in her throat. "I really appreciate this. I'll call you in a couple of hours."

She did still want that freedom. It was just pushed down further, because more immediately, her brothers needed her intervention, and a baby girl in want of her love. She had a feeling that all the freedom in the world wouldn't be half as satisfying if she knew she was letting down the ones she loved.

Chapter Eight

When Bryce got the baby back to the house—it was walking distance—he still wasn't sure why he'd volunteered to do this. His only thought was that he'd seen the look on Lily's face, and it was clear she was overwhelmed.

He had a feeling she was in the same position with her brothers at the moment—desperate to do something for them, but not sure what that looked like. They had more in common than he cared to admit, it seemed. Lily had needed someone to step up for her. Was it stupid of him to want to be that guy?

Babysitting Emily was the most obvious solution, temporary as it may be. Lily had family issues to deal with, and she'd be able to deal with them more effectively if she wasn't caring for an infant at the same time. Simple.

Or not so simple. He was now responsible for a newborn for the next few hours. Alone.

"Hello." He looked down into Emily's face. She was awake, big brown eyes fixed on his face. "It's you and me, kid."

She didn't answer. Obviously. He put the car seat onto the kitchen table and fixed her with a contemplative stare.

"This was a terrible idea," he said. "I'm sorry I got you into this."

She seemed as curious as he was about what was about to unfold. But he couldn't just leave her in a car seat, and pretty soon she'd probably want a bottle or something, so he went to the cupboard and pulled down a can of formula. It had instructions on the side—finally, something with some logical directions attached—and went about preparing a bottle.

"I'm not completely useless," he told the baby over his shoulder. "We'll figure this out until Lily gets back."

Those were his father's words coming out of his mouth. His dad had said the exact thing to him when he was about five and they'd been left in the house together. He didn't know where his mother had gone, but he still remembered his father looking down at him with a wrinkled brow saying, "I'm not completely useless, kid. We'll probably eat. That's something."

Famous words, because as it turned out, his father was pretty close to being useless, especially when he left a few months later. He walked out the door and never came back. And he'd never forgiven his dad for doing that, because Bryce had needed him. But if his father had stuck around, it never would have been a Norman Rockwell painting. His father hadn't paid much attention to him at the best of times. In fact, the only time he remembered doing anything with his dad was that one time the man had reassured him that they'd probably eat. There were a few old pictures in the family album of his father on the couch with a beer, his attention riveted to the television, and Bryce sitting on the floor in a diaper. In fact, every picture of the two of them together had his father looking in the other direction and Bryce just standing there in the general vicinity of the man who had sired him. Would he have had less to resent if his father had stayed, or just different things to resent?

Emily wriggled in the car seat and made a face.

"Okay, I'm coming," he said, and he undid the buckles just as the smell hit him. It was strong enough that his eyes watered. "Oh wow, Piglet... Wow..."

Diaper duty already. He'd avoided it at the station, and watched Lily do the honors at her aunt's house, but he'd naively hoped that he could avoid ever touching a diaper if he timed things right.

"Can that wait?" he asked her seriously. "I mean, do you need me to look into that, or can we just pretend it didn't happen?"

In response, Emily's face crumpled into a wail, and he heaved a sigh.

The actual changing of the diaper was a more traumatic event than anticipated. He used up an entire box of baby wipes and managed to get Emily's clothes soiled, as well as three bath towels and a spot on the carpet he wasn't sure he was going to be able to get out again... In total, it took half an hour, and Emily wet on his shirt before he managed to get her into a diaper again.

He was then too uncertain of his skills to even try dressing her in something clean, so he wrapped her in a tea towel and then sank into a recliner in the sitting room, the baby propped up on his shoulder.

She was tiny, her skin so soft, and she bobbed her head up and down a couple of times before settling her cheek against his shoulder and heaving a long sigh. She smelled of baby wipes and formula, and something sweet that he couldn't quite place. It was a nice smell, he decided.

I'm really bad at this. He knew it was true. He wasn't looking forward to explaining to Lily how the flower-patterned rug had gotten soiled. He'd offer to pay for the cleaning—it was the least he could do.

When he looked over at Emily, he saw her eyes slowly shut, a dribble of drool soaking into his shirt and wetting his shoulder.

For the moment, he would just sit. Very still. He'd let the baby sleep, and he wouldn't move a muscle. There was a TV across the room, but the remote lay on a couch cushion out of reach, so that wasn't much help.

Father, why do I feel like You're playing a joke on me?

He believed that all things happened for a reason, and when he was sent to Comfort Creek, he'd wondered if God was going to help him address his anger. He hadn't had his patience tested—not like it had been with Leroy Higgins. Instead, Bryce had been caring for a baby the entire time, and when he wasn't around Emily, he seemed to be thinking about her…and about Lily. So what was God trying to teach him out here in Comfort Creek? What had been the point of all of this?

He thought he'd had everything under control until Leroy started in on him. He'd gotten over Kelly, gotten into a good rhythm with work and friends. He'd even started volunteering more with his local church. He'd been okay. He hadn't been aching for something he couldn't have until he got to Comfort Creek and had a family stuck under his nose.

I want more, Lord, he prayed silently. *I want a wife*.

He could see what he'd been missing. A wife to wake up to, to come home to, to worry if he got off late. He wanted someone to go to church with, to sit next to in the pew where he could slide his arm around her and smell that soft scent of her perfume. In that mental image, she wore a cherry-patterned dress, and he shook his head, pulling himself out of it.

Lily wasn't the wife he needed. It didn't matter how sweet she was, or how funny. It didn't matter that he thought about her more than he should, or that she made him feel better about himself, somehow, just by being there. None of that mattered, because she was no different from the others—she wanted kids. That was a door closed.

Soon enough, Emily would be adopted by a family and she'd have real parents to love and protect her. She'd have a dad, and that man would be the one to teach her how to ride a bike, teach her how to make pancakes for supper and one day walk her down the aisle. She'd have a real father, not just a stand-in like him, and she deserved the real thing.

Emily wriggled in his arms, her little mouth opening in a small circle, a pink tongue coming out. He knew that look by now—she was hungry.

Bryce eased himself up out of the chair and headed to the kitchen, where the bottle waited on the counter where he'd left it. It took some maneuvering, but he soon got her into the right position for her feeding. He hoped that her forever father would see what he saw in this little girl—spirit and sweetness...and an appetite that made him grin.

Lord, let her new dad love her like crazy and protect her from the bad stuff. Bless him. Really bless him. Pour it on, Lord. Because Emily deserves the best father she can get.

As Lily eased up the drive toward her house, she was still uncertain about how productive her talk with the boys had been. As it turned out, her younger brothers were all pretty angry at Lily for having moved out. They missed her, and they didn't think it was fair that she got to start a new life without them. They'd never do that to her, they told her with chins quivering with rarely seen emotion. It was like she didn't care anymore.

And she'd had to explain that she hadn't left them, she'd just grown up. They'd move out, too, one day, and that didn't mean that she loved them any less, but they couldn't treat her new business like they'd treated her bedroom. She'd lose more than her investment if this bed-and-breakfast failed; she'd lose her livelihood. Her business wasn't like a box of cookies—it wasn't something to be shared by them all, and they had to respect that.

She thought that she'd gotten through to them a little bit, but they still hadn't warmed up entirely. They were angry, and bringing them all together into the same room only seemed to make them angrier because they were all feeling the same way. Her mother had talked to them about the dangers of underage drinking, and even of drinking at the legal age. Lily's grandfather had been an alcoholic, and so had Lily's father.

"Please," Lily had said quietly. "I love you guys.

Stop with the drinking and the risky behavior. I'll make more time for you, okay? If you want my attention, pick up the phone and call me, and we'll make plans. I promise."

She thought they'd made progress, but she couldn't be sure. Teenage boys could be hard to read at the best of times. She had hugged her mother before she left and thought about the discussion all the way home. And now that she'd pulled into the driveway, she felt a little more peaceful.

Lord, show me how to help them, she prayed silently. *And please protect them. Don't let them do anything too stupid!*

She got out of the car and headed up the walk to the front door. She paused, listening. All was quiet, which was a good sign…she hoped. She opened the door and came inside to find Bryce in the recliner, Emily on his chest, covered in what looked to be a tea towel.

"Hi," she said. "Were you sleeping?"

"She is, not me. I couldn't get her into the bassinet," he said. "I could use a hand."

Lily put her purse down by the door and picked up the baby in her arms. The tea towel fell aside, and she wrapped it around Emily once more, but she cast Bryce a curious look.

"It's a long story," Bryce said. "It involves that stain on the carpet. I'll pay for the cleaning."

"No need," she said, glancing at the stain. If it was what she thought it was, it would come right out. "Vinegar and water will do the trick."

"That's a relief." He pushed himself out of the recliner, and they made their way to the kitchen where the bassinet waited. Lily slipped Emily into it and pulled a blanket over her. Since Emily was sleeping, Lily would let the diaper wait. The baby let out a soft sigh and put one balled-up hand next to her face, but didn't awaken.

"It looks like you survived," she said, shooting him a smile. Whatever happened, it had resulted in a rather large pile of dirty clothes in the corner of the kitchen next to the laundry room, but she didn't want to ask. Emily stirred in her sleep.

"Barely." His tone was low, but the small smile betrayed more beneath the surface. He looked out the window toward the wooden framed swing. It had a bench seat that hung between an A-frame structure that served as a trellis for some errant morning glories, the flowers closed in rest as they did before sunlight coaxed them open again. Lily had spent many a morning on that swing with her Bible.

"So how did it go with the boys?" he asked.

"They're furious with me, but I think we're going in the right direction," she said, and the baby let out a little grunt in her sleep.

"Should we go outside so we don't wake her up?" he suggested.

It was a good idea, and Lily pushed open the kitchen window so that they'd hear any sounds Emily made. Then they eased out the side door into the cool night, and Lily sucked in a breath of lilac-scented air. The swing hung invitingly close. Lily sat first, and then Bryce eased in next to her, his arm brushing hers and emanating warmth against her. She lifted her feet and they hung suspended for a moment before Bryce pushed them back and then lifted his. The gentle rocking was soothing, and Lily heaved a quiet sigh. She was more tired than she'd thought.

"Thanks for watching her, Bryce."

"My pleasure."

Was it? She glanced toward him, and he didn't look half as frazzled as she expected. He shrugged and cast her a bashful smile.

"Piglet is pretty cute. What can I say?"

Piglet. Why he refused to let go of that nickname, she'd never know. The chains that held the swing creaked softly, and the cool evening air whisked her hair away from her forehead with each rush forward.

"So how did it go with your brothers?" he repeated his question from inside.

She was silent for a moment, considering her response. "I honestly don't know," she admitted. "They're furious with me."

"How come?"

"I left." She smiled sadly. "At least that's the way they see it. I was always there for them, like a second mother, almost, and then I moved out. They feel like I abandoned them."

"And they're trying to get your attention," he concluded.

"And succeeding." She smiled sadly. "I feel so guilty."

"Don't." He shrugged, and she felt the movement against her arm. "Starting your own life isn't wrong. But those adjustments aren't easy, either. For anyone, I guess."

"I know…" And she did recognize that. She couldn't just live with her mother until all the boys were grown with lives of their own. She wasn't willing to sacrifice her own life—her own future husband and kids, her own business—for their comfort. She loved them, but growing up with four younger siblings had meant that she'd had to give up her own fair share more often than not. They weren't her children, they were her brothers, and that made for a different dynamic, although one where she ended up equally riddled with guilt.

Bryce reached over and took her hand in his warm palm, giving her fingers a squeeze. "You'll figure it out."

"Thanks." She certainly hoped that was true. "They think they know so much."

Bryce chuckled. He didn't release her hand, and she was glad of that, because his strong grip made her feel stronger, too.

"I was a handful, too," he said. "And every time I took some huge risk, my mother would say the same thing to me..."

His voice trailed away, and when he didn't finish the thought, she prompted, "What would she say?"

He glanced down at her, humor laced with bitterness in his blue eyes. "That I'm just like my dad."

She felt the weight of those words, and she frowned slightly. "What did she mean by that?"

"I look like him, you know," he said, not seeming to answer to question, at least not directly. "If you see pictures of my father at my age, we're like twins."

So his father was a handsome man, too. She blushed a little when she realized where her thoughts had gone. It wasn't unheard of for a son to carry on family traits.

"Was he a real risk-taker or something?" she asked.

"Oh, definitely," Bryce replied. "You have to be in order to be a cop, and I followed in his footsteps. It takes a certain personality to strap on your gear and head out into the night. I think that scared her—that I was my father's carbon copy."

"You're half your mother, too," Lily pointed out.

"But she and I are different as night and day," Bryce replied. "She's fair, like you. And petite. She worries a lot—all the time, actually. She's serious."

"Don't boys want to be like their fathers?" she asked.

"Not me." He glanced down at her again, and his face was only inches away. Those gentle blue eyes met her gaze, and a sad smile turned up one side of his mouth. "I've been fighting it my whole life."

"Oh…" She whispered, and he leaned closer so that his arm pressed against hers, almost as if he found her comforting. Then he looked out into the yard, away from her, his fingers moving in slow circles over hers.

"My dad was almost charged with accepting bribes, but he quit and they dropped the charges because a witness backed out. Still, everyone thinks he did it."

She winced. That kind of fall from a pedestal would hurt a boy. There came a time when an adult recognized that their parents were human, but no one was fully at peace with a parent being morally corrupt. That sting never got better. Still, he might not think his father was guilty.

"But what do you think?" she asked.

"I think he did it."

She could feel the emotion in those words. She tipped her head against his strong shoulder and let out a slow breath.

"My dad was a drinker," she said. "He died in a car accident, and his blood alcohol level was four times the legal level. He wrapped the family car around a tree. We were all home, waiting for him to get back. Thankfully, no one else was killed because of his drinking and driving, but I do understand not wanting to turn out like your dad…"

"…or wanting to protect someone else from turning out just like him," he said.

"Except I'd never tell my brothers that they're just like my dad," she said. "That's too much for small shoulders."

"Do you think your brothers *will* be like him?" Bryce asked quietly.

Did she? It was most certainly her worry. Alcoholism ran in families, and theirs had a strong history of substance abuse. She'd vowed to never drink for that very reason, and seeing her brothers start drinking this young worried her…deeply. But there was a difference between her brothers and their father—her brothers had *her*.

"Over my dead body." She smiled wryly. "But the genes are there that make them prone to substance abuse. I'll admit that it scares me."

Bryce shifted his position and pulled his arm up and rested it on the back of the seat behind her shoulders. He was closer now, and she could make out the soft stubble on his chin and the worry lines around his eyes. He moved a wisp of hair away from her face, his fingers lingering for a moment against her skin. Then he dropped his hand.

"You're stronger than you think," he said quietly.

"I'm stronger than they think, too," she said with a wry smile.

He laughed softly, the sound low and close. The smile dropped from her face as she met his eyes again. He was so strong, so present…so tempting to lean into those muscular arms and rest her head on his shoulder one more time. But she couldn't allow herself to go there. She knew better than this...

Or she had at some very logical point in the near past. Right now, her mind wasn't functioning properly, and her thoughts swam around in a frustrating blur.

He brushed her hair away from her cheek, and this time, he didn't pull his hand back. The backs of his fingers lingered against her face, and his gaze met hers again. Those gentle eyes looked both softer and more insistent, and he leaned closer, so close that she could feel the whisper of breath against her lips. Her eyes fluttered shut, and his mouth pressed against hers. It was a soft kiss, tender and sweet. He didn't push for more, and she didn't pull away. It felt right—oh so right—even though her mind disagreed.

Just then, a sound broke the stillness—Emily's little cry from the kitchen.

Lily blinked her eyes open and pulled back.

"The baby—" she said, and in a rush, every single reason why she had no business kissing Bryce Camden flooded back into her mind. He didn't want this, and he wasn't staying. Bryce was here for another week, and then it would all go back to normal, and she didn't need to be nursing a broken heart when that happened.

She swallowed hard and rose to her feet, stepping away from him, trying to get her thoughts straightened out once more.

"I'll take her to the cottage now," Lily said, and she turned toward the door.

"Okay," he said, not moving from his position. "Good night, Lily."

Emily's cry tugged her toward the house, and when

she glanced back over her shoulder, she saw Bryce still seated on that swing, leaning his elbows on his knees and his shoulders stooped like they carried a burden heavier than she could imagine.

Chapter Nine

The next day, Bryce was irritable. He woke before dawn and spent some time with his Bible, but he still couldn't find that comfortable old groove he'd left behind. And he missed it—he missed knowing where he stood in life, and where he belonged, but this sensitivity training in Comfort Creek was turning him on his head in too many ways. He was feeling things he knew better than to feel, and he'd been thinking altogether too much about Lily. Even Piglet had managed to slip under his defenses.

He blamed the sleepy nature of this town. Nothing happened. There wasn't any distraction, at least not the criminal kind that he was so good at dealing with. Comfort Creek was dozily subversive.

He left the house before Lily came in to make breakfast, writing a quick note that he had a few things to take care of at the station. He propped it up in the center of the kitchen table where she'd see it, and even that gesture of consideration irritated him, because it made him picture what she'd look like when she found it, and it made him wonder what she'd think.

He'd kissed her last night under the stars. And then she'd dashed off. Had he scared her? Had he shocked her?

That rankled him. He knew better than to kiss Lily. He wasn't here to get attached. He was here to do his time and get out. So why would he allow himself to toy with Lily's feelings like that? She was worth more than he could offer, and he'd never been the kind of man to mess with a woman's emotions. He might be a lot of things—and an awful lot like his old man—but he was not a player.

At this moment, Bryce sat at his temporary desk doing a bit of paperwork, or at least going through the motions. The coffeemaker burbled from across the bullpen, a sound he could only hear because the station was still mostly empty. There were some day-old doughnuts on the counter that he'd looked over dubiously when he'd come in. He'd eaten two—he wasn't that picky, but he was very aware that he was probably missing out on a delicious meal back at the house.

The chief came out of the station's gym in full uniform. There were showers and lockers inside so that the officers could get a workout first thing in the morning. Bryce had considered it, but retreated when he saw the chief pumping weights. Now Chief Morgan headed across the bullpen past where Bryce sat.

"Morning," Chief Morgan said, pausing at his desk. "You're in early."

"Yeah." Bryce gave the man a nod. Bryce suppressed a grimace when the other man regarded him for a moment, then pulled up a chair. The chief looked to be a little less than forty, but he seemed wiser than his years. And while Bryce liked him, he wasn't exactly interested in being buddies—hence skipping his own workout this morning.

"So how is the baby doing?" the chief asked.

Bryce scribbled his signature at the bottom of a form. "She's good. She can still empty a bottle in no time. Nearly killed me with a diaper the other day."

Morgan chuckled. "Don't envy you that."

A couple of days ago, he might have agreed, but it was as though being in the trenches with the kid had given them a bit of bond…and a story. He felt like he was letting Piglet down if he didn't stand up for her a bit.

"She's cute, though," Bryce amended. The baby liked him, and while he sincerely believed that Piglet could improve on her taste in men, it warmed him that she was so cozy when snuggled against his chest.

"Yeah…" Chief Morgan nodded. "So, I got a call from the FBI last night."

Bryce froze. His friend was supposed to call him back, not pass it up the ladder, but maybe he hadn't had much choice. He narrowed his eyes and met the chief's gaze, waiting.

"They confirmed that Aaron Bay is not in the witness protection program," the chief went on. "Anything you wanted to tell me about?"

"Just looking into things for Lily Ellison," Bryce admitted. "Her aunt is marrying the guy, and she's got a bad feeling about it. Her aunt is in her sixties, and this guy is twenty years younger. It might be nothing. I'm just…poking around."

He half expected Chief Morgan to tell him to drop it and send him into the roomful of binders, but instead, he looked down at the desk, nodding slowly and chewing one side of his cheek. Finally he said, "So what did you find?"

"Zero," Bryce shrugged. "As in, his slate is too clean."

"I know Clarisse Clifton," he said. "She gave me piano lessons when I was a kid. A good lady, well loved."

"Have you met her fiancé?" Bryce asked.

"No," the chief admitted. "What's he like? What does your gut tell you?"

Bryce went over the man in his head, looking for some way of summing him up. "Gentle. Faded. I can't get a good read on him. It's kind of a flatline. I don't know what to think, but I can tell you this much, he doesn't have any ID except for a Colorado driver's license."

"So we need to see the ID that got him that license," Chief Morgan surmised.

"That's my thinking, sir."

"I could expedite that a bit for you." The chief tapped the desk and rose to his feet. "Drop the information you've got on my desk, and I'll see what I can do."

Bryce nodded. "Thanks, sir. I appreciate it."

Chief Morgan didn't walk away, though, and he eyed Bryce curiously. "Is this one personal for you, Camden?"

Was it? Bryce had started looking into this as a favor for his hostess. Truthfully, he'd felt a little bad for her because she'd been so open and friendly, and if he said no to her impetuous request, it would have seemed like a rebuff, and the last thing he had wanted to do was push her away.

"It's, uh—" Bryce wasn't sure how to answer. "It's

personal to Miss Ellison, sir, and I guess that's good enough for me."

Chief Morgan nodded his head slowly, then let out a long breath. "Okay, then. I'm around if you want to talk."

Bryce wasn't sure what the man meant by that, but he headed off in the direction of his office, leaving Bryce in momentary peace, and that's exactly what he was wanting. Except, some good old-fashioned police work was even better, and his mind was already chewing over the Aaron Bay problem.

Who was he? And why were there no bread crumbs leading away from this guy? Why was it so hard to dig up anything on him? He wasn't in the witness protection program, which took away some of the complications to do with his history, but it only led to more questions.

He glanced at his watch. It was almost time for him to start his morning patrol, but he still had some time to check in with Lily and give her the information he'd learned so far. He didn't like the way he woke up at the thought of speaking with her—like she was a little shot of caffeine to his system. He'd need to sort that out privately, but until then…

He pulled out his cell phone and dialed her number. It rang twice, and then she picked up.

"Hello?"

"Hi, Lily, it's Bryce."

"Hi!" She sounded cheerful enough, but there was a little bit of caution in her voice, too, and he closed his eyes and grimaced.

"I know I kind of ran out early this morning—"

"No, no, it's fine."

"Last night, I—"

"It's okay, no need—"

"No, really…"

This was ridiculous. They were both uncomfortable, and this obviously wasn't something they could talk about over the phone.

"Let's not talk about that now," he suggested, and he could hear her audible sigh of relief.

"That's a good idea." She sounded more like herself now.

"So what did I miss out on for breakfast?" he asked, keeping his voice low and turning his back on the bullpen to maintain a little privacy from the officers who were filtering into the station now.

"French toast with fresh strawberries and maple syrup," she replied.

His stomach rumbled at the very thought. "I'm regretting missing that."

"Good." He could hear the smile in her voice.

"Look, I checked into Aaron Bay a little more. I was curious to see if he was part of the witness protection program, and it turns out he isn't."

"That would have been a great excuse for him," she said.

"Yeah." He felt the smile come to his face in spite of himself. "But that does leave us with more questions."

"That reminds me," she said. "I have some of the women from the family coming over tonight to put together some last-minute place cards for the wedding. I don't have room to have them all in my cottage, and—"

He could hear the regret in her voice. She really did want to make her establishment purely professional, but a place like Comfort Creek didn't seem to allow for that very easily.

"Hey, it's no problem," he said. "Desperate times, desperate measures."

"And one week until the wedding," she said.

His smile dropped. One week. One week until Clarisse and Aaron were married, and one week until he left town. The two-week stint out here had sounded like an eternity when he arrived, and already it was feeling too short for him to wrap up the loose threads that were unraveling around him.

"I'm not done looking into Aaron yet. I'll see what I can unearth," he promised.

"If you're interested in that French toast," Lily said, "I can leave some in the fridge for you."

"Oh, I don't want to put you out," he said.

"It's no bother. I'm making it for myself anyway." Her voice was so guileless, and he had no doubt that she was fully intending to enjoy a leisurely breakfast whether her guest was around or not. And he was glad of it. Why shouldn't she enjoy the delectable meals she provided her guests? But he couldn't help but wonder what her plans were for the food if he didn't want it...

"What about your brothers?" he asked suddenly. Were the boys hungry this morning? He wasn't sure why he suddenly so concerned with their eating habits, but he was.

"I picked up some groceries for them yesterday," she said. "They're taken care of."

He nodded. "Okay, well, I'd love that French toast. I'll see when I can stop by later on. Will you be around?"

"I'll be out this morning, actually," she said. "My aunt is going to a wedding dress fitting, and that falls under maid of honor duties. So I'll have it in the fridge for you. I'll leave the key under the rock beside the front door."

"Isn't that really obvious?" he asked.

"Well, I wanted you to be able to find it. Trust me, no one is going to break in. But if that rankles you so much, I can put it on top of the door frame."

"That's another really obvious place." He felt a wry smile come to his lips. "That's as bad as under the mat." He was enjoying this a little bit. She was silent for a moment, and he could hear her breathing softly through the phone. What was it about her that even listening to her breathe made him feel calmer in spite of himself?

"I'll stick it under the seat of the garden swing in the backyard with a piece of sticky tack." She sounded self-satisfied with that answer, and he grinned.

"Perfect." And his mind immediately went back to the last time they sat on that swing together. He pulled his thoughts firmly away. "Chief Morgan is looking into Aaron's trail, too, so I'll let you know the minute we come up with something."

"Thanks, Bryce." Her tone was gentle and grateful. It was that combination that slid right past all his defenses so easily and brought that goofy grin to his face.

"No problem. Have fun with your aunt."

When he hung up, he was motionless for a moment, staring at his phone. He needed to get his mind off of her, but everything in this town reminded him of her in some way. Comfort Creek was supposed to be punishment, but it was turning into a whole new kind of torture he'd never anticipated. It might have been easier if they'd just kept him in Fort Collins and sat him next to the most intriguing woman they could find for a couple of weeks straight, then told him to keep it strictly professional. Except he had a feeling that even if they'd tried, they couldn't have some up with a woman to match Lily Ellison.

This had been the cruelest coincidence of his life.

Blessings Bridal Boutique was located just north of Main Street on Sycamore Drive. It was a small building at the front that opened up into a larger display area in the back, and it had catered to Comfort Creek's brides for the last sixty years. Harper Kemp ran the store now, and it had been in her family since it opened.

When Lily and Aunt Clarisse arrived, they parked in the back and ambled around the side of the aging building toward the front door.

"I bought my first wedding dress here," Clarisse said. She shot her niece a smile that was tinged with sadness. "Everyone bought their dresses here. It was either Blessings Bridal or the city. You had to really plan back then if you wanted a real wedding dress. You had to give the Kemps enough time to make it or to order it in. We didn't rush a wedding back then unless there was good reason or there was a dress a girl could borrow from a married sister or cousin."

Her aunt had been rambling on about the way it used to be the entire drive over. Lily knew Clarisse didn't mean anything by it, but she couldn't help but ask, "And why the rush now, Auntie?"

They stopped in front of the store. At this end of the street, the storefronts melted into houses, and right next to the bridal shop stood an old, rambling three-story house that had seen better days. Sunlight filtered down through the branches of mature trees that stretched overhead.

"Oh, I'm not getting a gown," Clarisse said with a wave of her hand, as if that made everything different. "I've done that once already, and at my age, I don't need to look like a blushing bride. I'm a grown woman who knows her mind—that's the look I'm going for." Clarisse shot Lily an exultant smile. "And when you fall in love one of these days, I'll return the favor."

"What favor?" Lily asked with a laugh.

"I'll reserve judgment," Clarisse replied, shooting Lily an arch look, then pulled open the front door to Blessings Bridal.

A bell tinkled overhead, and they stepped into the shop. One thing was clear—Aunt Clarisse wasn't going to accept any dampening of her happiness. A wriggle of worry wormed its way up inside Lily's stomach. If Aaron was a con man, Clarisse would be crushed.

Harper Kemp was a slim, redheaded woman of almost thirty. She wore tortoiseshell glasses, and her hair was twisted up in a loose bun on the top of her head, a few curls coming loose. She poked a pen behind her ear when they entered, and she came out from behind the counter.

"Good morning, ladies!" she said with a smile. "This is an exciting day, isn't it? I can't wait to see you in this dress, Clarisse. I think we've managed perfection this time."

Aunt Clarisse's cheeks grew pink and she folded her hands in front of her. "Well, I'd like to look respectable."

"You'll look more than respectable," Harper replied

with a smile of pure delight. "You'll be beautiful. I'll be right back with your dress."

Harper disappeared, and Clarisse looked over at Lily with a nervous smile. "I hope you like it."

Lily had never stood in this bridal shop before. She'd never been a bride or a bridesmaid and had no reason to come inside. Yet being here made her aunt's wedding seem so much more concrete. This was happening—and very soon.

And yet her mind wasn't completely on her aunt's wedding, either. She was still going over that kiss in her mind—the feeling of Bryce's soft lips pressed against hers. If he'd been pushy, more insistent, she'd never have kissed him back, but his gentle kiss that asked for nothing more...

She pulled mind back to the present.

"Of course I'll love it," Lily said. "Wow. It feels so real, doesn't it?"

"The last time I was here," Clarisse said softly, "for myself, that is, I was terrified. Three days before I came into this shop to start looking at dresses, your uncle Earl had called off the wedding."

"What?" Lily eyed her aunt curiously.

"I didn't tell anyone," she said with a shake of her head. "It lasted one night, and the next morning we made up and our plans continued, but when I came into this shop to choose a dress, I have to confess, I was terrified that something would happen and Earl and I wouldn't get married after all. I mean, if he could get cold feet once, right?"

"But obviously, you did get married," Lily pointed out.

"Oh yes, we did. I found out later that my father had a talk with Earl and told him that they were putting down money on the dress and if he wasn't going to be man enough to get married, then now was the time to back out. Earl told my father he was committed. So my father took me dress shopping and we chose a gown that very day. He put down the deposit in cash and I remember I'd never seen so much money at one time..."

Lily remembered the pictures from her aunt's sitting room. They were faded color prints of the wedding where Clarisse was slim and petite and Earl was lanky and gangly-looking. Clarisse beamed up at her brand-new husband in those photos, wearing a lace gown with a long train. Clarisse and Earl hadn't been able to have children, but their hearts were big enough for all their nieces and nephews.

"But this time," Clarisse said, "it's different."

Lily looked at her aunt curiously. "Because you've been married before?"

"I know what to expect this time," Clarisse agreed, "but I'm not afraid that he'll change his mind and bolt on me. I'd never been so relieved than when Earl actually said the words *I do*. But with Aaron, it just feels different. I'm more secure, I suppose."

Lily didn't know what to say. She'd never been married herself, and she had no words of wisdom for a bride more than twice her age. What she wanted to say was "Be careful, Auntie! He might not be what you think he is," but she didn't dare. Not here. She was saved from thinking up an answer by Harper returning with a plastic-covered dress on a hanger.

The dress was ivory silk and looked to be tea length with a fitted skirt. It had a sash of pearl pink at the waist and a little sleeved jacket that went with it. When Clarisse saw it, she let out a shaky sigh. It was a beauti-

ful dress—perfect for her aunt and for the occasion—
and Lily couldn't help the mist that rose in her eyes.

"Wow," Lily whispered. "I love it."

"How do you feel, Clarisse?" Harper asked.

Clarisse fingered the material tenderly. "Like a
bride," she said softly.

"Now we just need to see you in it," Harper said,
dropping the plastic over the dress once more. "Shall
we?"

The women disappeared into a changing room, and
Lily stood in the center of the store, her eyes moving
over the dresses on display. Her mind was still most
firmly on that kiss. She shouldn't have done it—she
had a choice in the matter, too. She should have said
something noble and definitive about her role as his
hostess and how they both knew he was leaving... But
all thoughts had drained from her head looking into
those ice-blue eyes.

She paused in front of a dress, looking at it wistfully. She had trouble seeing her own wedding in her
thoughts about the future. That part was blurry, but
she could imagine herself later on, after the wedding,
when she and her guy settled into regular life. She'd
be running the bed-and-breakfast, and her husband
would come home after work in the evening and play
with the kids in the backyard while she finished up
some canning. They'd be Mr. and Mrs. and the Comfort Creek Bed-and-Breakfast would be a joint venture.
When she imagined what her Mr. might look like, for
some reason, the face that kept popping into her mind
was Bryce's. She blushed when she realized what she
was doing.

It was that kiss. *Just a kiss*, she reminded herself.

Neither of them had been thinking straight, obviously, and she couldn't make more of it than that.

Not him, she told herself firmly, and when her imagination wouldn't comply, she pushed the thoughts away.

One of the main dresses on display was a white dress with a tulle princess skirt. The bodice was worked with silver thread and tiny pearl beads. It was stunning—much more adventurous than Lily would ever wear, but still, it drew her eye and her curious fingertips. If she were getting married, would she allow herself the luxury of trying on such a dress? Or would she go straight to the dresses she could legitimately afford? Being the practical woman she was, she'd likely stick to her budget with the tenacity she showed for most decisions in her life.

The changing room opened, and Lily pulled her fingers away as if they'd been burned and put her hands behind her back. She didn't know why she felt so wrong about touching the dress. Surely, many a bride had touched that particular dress in her perusal of the store, but Lily wasn't here as a bride. She was here for her aunt.

Aunt Clarisse stood in front of a three-paneled mirror, and Lily couldn't help but smile at the sight of her. Aunt Clarisse, who always looked most comfortable in an apron, suddenly looked every inch a bride.

The ivory material skimmed over Clarisse's ample curves, ending midcalf. The pink sash accentuated her waistline, and the little jacket brought the whole look together in a neat, elegant package. On her head, she wore a faux diamond fascinator with a spray of gauzy veil that slipped down over her forehead. Harper handed her a show bouquet to hold, and when Clarisse turned to face Lily, she had to swallow back the lump in her throat.

"You look gorgeous," Lily breathed. "Really, truly… just beautiful!"

"When is the big day?" Harper asked.

"This weekend," Clarisse said, turning back to the mirror, and Lily felt her stomach drop.

This was all fine and good to see her aunt so happy and beautiful, but after that wedding day, real life would continue. If Aaron had ulterior motives, then Bryce had very little time left to dig up the truth.

Lord, she prayed silently, *if there is something we need to know, please let us find it. And please don't let him break my aunt's heart.*

Chapter Ten

That evening, Bryce stood in the doorway of the kitchen, watching as Lily's female family members pored over a seating chart, scissors and various crafting supplies held aloft as they worked. A huge poster board lay on the kitchen table next to some rectangles of card stock, metallic pens and various decorations to be glued in place. They were working on place cards to be used during the reception.

One of the older women cradled Piglet in her arms, looking lovingly down into her sleeping face as if the mayhem around her wasn't even happening. That was the life, when you could sleep through such chaos. Piglet had it better than she realized.

Lily paused next to Bryce, a plate of cookies in one hand. She wore a pair of jeans and a blue blouse that set off her eyes—not that Bryce would mention it. He'd wanted to talk to her about that evening on the swing, but everyone had arrived already before he got off his shift, and there hadn't been a chance. Maybe that was for the best, after all. If they could just move past it, pretend it hadn't happened, maybe it would actually be like it hadn't happened. Did that ever work?

The plate of fragrant chocolate chip cookies in Lily's hands drew Bryce's attention, and he nabbed a couple of them as they watched the women argue.

"You absolutely cannot put Bruce next to Ian," Lily's mother, Iris, was saying. "They'll come to blows. Seriously. What are you thinking?"

"They're grown men!" another woman shot back. "It's forty-five minutes of their time, and they can fill their mouths with food."

"Ian will arrive drunk, you know that," Iris retorted.

"So where should we put him? He has to be as far from Bernice and Karl as possible…"

Iris looked a good deal like her daughter—older and more mature, obviously, but she had the same delicate cheekbones and an identical smile. Her hair was ash blond, and this evening she wore it pulled back into a ponytail, and she still wore the supermarket uniform from work.

"They're a force to be reckoned with," Bryce murmured.

"That they are," Lily agreed softly, then she chuckled. "Sometimes it's better to just back away and let them at it."

Bryce took a bite of the cookie and heaved a sigh of momentary contentment. Could she ever bake! These cookies were better than his own mother's, and that was saying something.

"We haven't found out anything more about Piglet's mom," Bryce said quietly. "She just…disappeared."

Lily sighed. "It's hard to imagine. I'm already

so attached. I don't even want to give her up to Bev Starchuck when she gets back in a few days."

He could see Lily's love for the baby in the way in the little things—like how she ran her fingers over Piglet's tiny hands, or how she played with that shock of black hair.

"We'll keep looking, of course," Bryce added.

"I know…" She didn't sound like that reassured her at all.

"So, have you found out anything more about Aaron?" Lily asked.

That's right. Back to his reason for being here in this kitchen—the suspicious fiancé.

"I talked to the chief, and he says that he hasn't gotten anything yet, but he understands the time pressure here."

"Okay…" She frowned, nodded. He wished he could do something to relieve her anxiety over this wedding. But he couldn't speed this up any more than he already had.

"If it turns out that Aaron is a con," Lily said, after a moment, "it'll be awful for Clarisse. I saw her in her wedding dress today, and if you could see the way her eyes lit up when she saw that dress—"

"Hey, it isn't like you're fabricating any of this," Bryce said quietly. "We're just looking into it."

"Then why do I feel so guilty?"

"Because you're sensitive," he replied with a shrug, and her gaze snapped up toward him. "Seriously. That's the reason why. Sensitive people often feel guilt for things that they aren't responsible for just because they are close enough to feel the discomfort of others. This isn't on you, Lily. You haven't done anything, and if the worst should turn out to be true, it still won't have anything to do with you."

He'd seen it often enough in his line of work. He was a first responder who dealt with people at the worst times of their lives. The people who often felt the worst about a situation were the bystanders who had no control over anything. But witnessing another's distress stabbed them deeply.

As a cop, he'd had to learn how to talk himself out of that kind of response. He was there to help. There were bad guys to blame for bad things. He couldn't allow himself to feel illogical guilt because he'd witnessed the fallout of someone else's crime. But that said, if Aaron turned out to be anything less than a Boy Scout, he'd take some personal pleasure in making sure he paid for any misery he put that sweet woman through. He might not know Clarisse Clifton beyond one evening spent at her home, but he could see how much Lily loved her. She didn't deserve to have her heart mangled.

"And who are these people?" someone asked, pointing at the dog-eared list.

"His family," Iris replied. "Of course."

"Well, who needs to be separated among them?"

All eyes turned to Lily. "None, apparently."

There were a few eye rolls.

"So what makes them so perfect?" one woman asked with a huff. "No one needs to be seated separately? They have no friction, these people?"

"Can I see that?" Bryce asked, and Iris glanced at him curiously.

"Sure." She passed it over, but she didn't take her eyes off of him as he glanced down the list of last names. There wasn't one Bay in the list, but if these were Aaron's family members, then this was a clue into his identity.

He smiled and handed it back. He'd love to copy it down, but he couldn't—not until the women had left—but this could speed up their investigation.

Piglet started to squirm and fuss, and the woman holding her put her up onto her shoulder and started to rub and pat her back soothingly. The older woman looked like a pro to him, but Piglet wasn't having it.

"Lily?" the older woman asked.

Lily now stood by the stove, wearing a pair of oven mitts as she pulled out another tray of cookies.

"Hand her to Bryce, would you?" Lily said. "He's got the touch with her."

All the women's eyes turned to Bryce now; he felt heat rise in his cheeks. What was it about this roomful of women that made him feel like a ten-year-old with his hand in the cookie jar? They regarded him in surprise for a moment, but when she passed him the baby, Piglet settled right down and snuggled against his chest.

"Well, I'll be..." Iris said.

"Huh," the aunt said with an incredulous shake of her head. "What do you make of that?"

All eyes turned to Lily now, and her cheeks bloomed pink. She looked helplessly from Bryce to her family.

"I don't know," she said shaking her head. "She likes him."

There was silence.

"He's actually quite charming, you know," she added.

Was he? He liked hearing her say that. In her eyes,

he seemed bigger, stronger, better somehow, than he was in a mirror. Charming—he'd never have billed himself that way, but he liked the sound of it coming from her. Lily shook her head and laughed.

"Oh, for crying out loud," she said. "Let's finish up this seating plan and get those place cards finished. I'm supposed to be running a business here."

As if Lily could even argue professionalism right now with her boarder holding the baby. The women, thankfully, turned back to their work of seating arrangements, and Bryce looked down at Piglet fondly.

"Hey, you," he whispered. "Did you miss me or something?"

Piglet blinked up at him, then her eyes drifted shut once more. He couldn't help but feel a little smug about her preference for him. He'd kind of missed her, too, if he had to admit to it. That wasn't a good thing—it would make his goodbye that weekend that much harder—but he was glad he'd met the tiny girl.

Lily stood at the stove scooping cookies off the pan with a spatula and depositing them onto a plate. She worked with expert ease, her hands seeming to know what to do. She was beautiful—even more so when she was focused on a job she enjoyed, like this one. He could see her happiness in the way she held herself, the way her shoulders were squared and the way her eyes shone.

She lifted the last cookie onto her spatula, then her gaze moved in his direction and she held the baked good toward him wordlessly. He shifted Piglet in his arms to free a hand and took the warm cookie off the spatula. He blew on it—it was more than warm now that it was in his hands—and took a gooey bite.

"Thanks," he said past the bite of cookie in his cheek.

Her response was a smile, but it sparkled in her eyes, and she turned again toward the table of ladies.

Stop enjoying this, he told himself gruffly. *This isn't yours*.

The baby in his arms, the beautiful woman across the kitchen, the family arguing at the table—none of this was his. It was tempting in a way he'd never felt before, even with Kelly, but it was firmly out of reach. And he'd best remember it. This was a closed door.

The evening wore on. Lily tucked Emily into her little bassinet and put it into the other room where it was quieter and she could sleep away from the strong kitchen lights. Bryce asked for the list of Aaron's family members, and she'd slipped it to him before he headed upstairs to his room.

Lily had some leftover cookies that she'd slid into the fridge out of sight so that she could send them home to her brothers. They'd know that she thought of them.

It had been a productive couple of hours. The seating arrangements were finalized to everyone's satisfaction, the place cards were finished up, and they'd gone over last-minute preparations for the ceremony. If this wedding didn't happen, there was going to be a lot of wasted work that had gone into it.

But Lily wouldn't complain about that if it meant saving her aunt from being conned by a criminal.

If that's even the case... Lord, please don't let me get carried away on this. Give me some perspective.

"So what do you think of Aaron?" her mother asked, drawing her attention back.

"He's—" How was she supposed to say this delicately? "He *seems* really nice."

"He seems really young," her aunt retorted, and the other women chuckled.

"Seems?" her mother prodded quietly.

"I don't know what to say," Lily confessed. "I went with Aunt Clarisse for her wedding dress fitting today, and seeing her like that—"

"What sort of dress is it?"

The conversation was sidelined then by discussion of wedding dresses for women Clarisse's age, and Lily gratefully let the topic slide. Her mother exchanged a look with her, though, which told Lily that Iris wasn't so easily put off. Everyone had an opinion, and everyone had some worries.

Except Clarisse herself.

Lily's cell phone rang, and she excused herself to the next room to pick up the call. It wasn't a number she recognized.

"Hello?"

"Hello, is this Lily Ellison?"

"Yes, speaking."

"Hi, this is Carol Goetz from children's services…"

Lily's gaze flew to the bassinet where Emily slept peacefully, the sound of the women in the next room chattering about the appropriateness of white for a second-time bride not bothering her in the least. Was her time with Emily going to end so quickly? Her heart constricted at the thought.

"…I was just calling to let you know that Beverly Starchuck is able to take over temporary custody of Baby Doe starting at nine a.m. tomorrow," Carol went on blithely.

Baby Doe. That's what the paperwork would call her, because she'd been left without a name, without a mother and without an identity. Except that Lily had gotten to know her rather well these last few days, and it seemed so faceless and empty to refer to her as Baby Doe, as if no one knew her.

"Her name is Emily," Lily said.

"No, Beverly Starchuck," the woman said, misunderstanding. "Let me double-check. Yes, Beverly."

"No, I'm saying that I've named the baby Emily," Lily said. "She needed a name."

"Oh…" Carol chuckled. "Okay, I'll make a note of that. It's a little nicer to say than Baby Doe, isn't it? So if you'd like to bring Baby…I mean, Emily, to Beverly's residence tomorrow, I can give you the address—"

This was how the arrangement was supposed to work. She'd agreed to take an infant for a very temporary situation. She'd confirmed with the police chief to make sure of that before she'd agreed to it. She had a brand-new business to run, and she couldn't be caring for an infant indefinitely…or could she? She'd been handling things so far. Granted, Bryce had helped out in the situation, but that didn't mean she couldn't have taken care of this…

Not that this was even an issue of Lily being able to care for Emily; it was an issue of Lily wanting to or not.

"Miss Ellison?" Carol said. "Are you there?"

"Yes, I'm here," Lily said. "I'm sorry about that."

"Shall I repeat the address for you?"

"No, I know Bev personally. I know where she lives," Lily said. "But I wasn't ready to give Emily up yet. I was wondering what options there are."

In the other room, the women burst into laughter

about something, and Lily moved farther away from the kitchen and toward the sitting room window. Outside, the sun had already set and the sky was a dusky pink, and she felt a wave of hopefulness rise up inside her. Was she crazy to be doing this?

"Well, Beverly is skilled in these sorts of situations," Carol said. "We need a foster care provider who is willing to meet with prospective adoptive families. This would be a considerable time demand—"

"No," Lily said quickly, the words flowing before she had a chance to second-guess them. "I mean I want to keep Emily. I'd like to… I'd like to adopt her myself."

"Oh!" Surprise registered in Carol's tone, and there was a pause. "Well, there is certainly no reason why you couldn't pursue adoption yourself. And since you are already her caregiver, we could simply extend your custody a little longer while you investigate your options with a lawyer…"

They talked a little while longer, but Lily's heart was soaring. This was an actual possibility! She could keep Emily, raise her as her own. Why say goodbye to a little girl who had so completely taken over her heart? Emily needed someone to love her like a mother would, and Lily could most definitely offer that. While there were no guarantees and the process was a lengthy one, Lily wasn't discouraged in the least.

"Thank you," Lily said as they finished their discussion. "I appreciate all the information, and I'll make sure I submit those forms in the next couple of days."

She hung up the phone just as Emily started to fuss in the bassinet. Lily went over to the baby's side and scooped her up, snuggling her close.

"We might not have to say goodbye, after all, sweetheart," she whispered. "I'm going to try to keep you. I want to be your mommy."

As she held Emily close and the baby snuggled up against her neck, it felt right—more than right, it felt perfect. But then something occurred to her that dampened her spirits. She hadn't prayed about this. She'd plunged forward on gut instinct, and she hadn't once put this before God. This was a massive decision, and she wasn't one to make that kind of decision without His guidance.

Lord, she prayed, *I jumped ahead there and I'm sorry. I should have stopped and asked You about this, but I want to keep her so badly. If this isn't Your will, close the doors quickly...* Her heart clenched at that thought, but she wouldn't turn from it, either. Sometimes God wanted different things for His children than they wanted for themselves, and she would be obedient to His will. When He said no, it hurt, but plunging ahead without God was worse.

But if You would allow me the honor of raising this child, I promise You that I'll love her and make her my first priority on this earth for as long as I live.

Whatever happened, God would be by her side, she knew that. For now, that would have to do. Faith was not easy—faith was not painless, either. Sometimes obedience could break a heart in two.

Chapter Eleven

The next day, Bryce did his best to get back into a Fort Collins frame of mind, but it was difficult while patrolling the sleepy streets of Comfort Creek. He'd made his rounds past the two-story brick high school with the flag flapping in the warm June wind. Then he turned down by the elementary school where teachers seemed to have given up because every time he passed the building, the playground was full of children and the sports field beside it had groups of kids doing outdoor activities. Then he'd turn back and circle around to Main Street, past the pub that always had a few trucks in the parking lot, no matter what time of day. Comfort Creek had a soothing quality about it, a geographical equivalent of a lullaby. But he didn't want to be lulled.

Last night, he'd turned in early for a reason—he'd felt himself slipping. This was Lily's town and Lily's family, and he'd found himself wanting to fit into it all, and that set off the warning bells. He'd gone up to his bedroom, pulled out that little notebook and written in block letters: *Pretending I belong with her.* He hated writing that one down, but it was penance. This was like a confession of sorts, and while he'd held back a good amount from this notebook, he'd give the chief this one. The worst part was that while he probably wasn't fooling any of the locals about how well he fit in, he'd been pretty effectively fooling himself, slipping into a role with Lily and the baby that he had no right to take on. And that was why needed his space.

That morning, Bryce had received two emails: one from the police chief setting up a meeting to go over his notebook of lies, and a second from his father.

Bryce, I heard about the disciplinary actions. I know how that feels. Give me a call if you want to talk.

That had been it—just a quick note offering a listening ear, which would be totally normal coming from any other father and being written to any other son. Why did his father always make these gestures at Bryce's lowest points in his life? Or was that the point—his father felt closest to him when he hit rock bottom?

Still the phone number was there, and Bryce had started dialing twice already, before hanging up. Did he want to talk to his father? But that was what Comfort Creek was all about, wasn't it—airing out his emotional closets?

As he slowed for a stop sign, he glanced out the open window at a corner store a few blocks from the high school. He'd expected to see a few students there, but he was surprised to recognize one of them—Lily's brother Randy. He sat on the curb, an open pop bottle in front of him on the cement and a chocolate bar in hand.

Bryce could have driven on, but Randy's expression gave him pause. He looked sad, and somehow that glum expression slipped past his personal armor.

He wasn't supposed to care—not too much, at least. He wasn't supposed to get involved, either. Randy wasn't doing anything wrong, and for all he knew he had a free period in school, but against all his better instincts, he had started to care in spite of himself. Hauling some kids off a fence and then not arresting them for an attempted break-and-enter had a way of turning him into a softy, apparently.

He sighed irritably and signaled a turn. Randy didn't wander off when Bryce pulled up, but he did shoot him an irritated glare.

"Morning," Bryce said.

"What?" Randy asked flatly. "Nice ride, by the way."

Bryce glanced at the offending minivan. Yeah, he couldn't blame the kid for that one. He came around to where Randy sat and regarded him in silence for a moment. Then he eased down onto the curb next to him.

"Skipping school?" Bryce asked.

"Nope." Randy smiled smugly and took a sip of pop, but didn't elaborate. "Go ahead and tell my sister."

"She worries about you," Bryce said.

"She shouldn't." Randy pulled a phone out of his pocket and read a text. He typed a reply, then put it between his feet. Bryce could see the text, even though Randy seemed to be trying to shield it with his foot. It was a text from a girl—Jen—who was in math class and was "sooooo bored" and missed Randy like crazy, followed by a googly-eyed emoji. His girlfriend, probably. Brycc could sympathize. He'd been sixteen once.

"Lily said you guys have been pretty stretched financially," Bryce said.

"That's nothing new," Randy retorted.

"How do you afford the phone?" Bryce asked.

"Pay as you go. It'll turn off tomorrow," Randy replied with a shrug. "What do you care?"

Bryce pulled a couple of twenties out of his pocket and passed them over.

"What's this for?" Randy asked with a suspicious frown, but he took the money anyway and tucked it away quickly.

"To keep your phone working," Bryce said.

"Thanks," Randy mumbled. "Appreciate it."

They sat in silence for a few minutes more, and then Randy broke the stillness.

"I wasn't going to steal anything at my sister's place. She told me what it looked like we were doing, but that wasn't it."

Bryce nodded, but didn't say anything. He had a feeling that Randy wanted to talk, and he was going to let him. Sometimes a kid just needed to feel heard once in a while—especially a kid with no dad at home. Bryce had been that kind of kid who hid his loneliness behind a bad attitude.

"I thought she was living it up while we were surviving on mac and cheese," Randy said, barking out a bitter laugh. "But Mom said that Lily's been giving her extra grocery money, and Mom didn't put it into food because she wanted to buy the twins phones, too, so that she can check on them easier."

"Phones are kind of a necessity these days," Bryce agreed.

"Yeah, well, I guess I didn't know what was going on, and I shouldn't have done all that."

"Lily really loves you guys," Bryce said. "You've got it good. I never had any brothers or sisters to get on my nerves. Wish I had."

Randy smiled for the first time. "Yeah, she's okay, I guess. I think we give her a hard time. She never does anything stupid. She's always so straitlaced. I wish she'd mess up just once to prove she's human!"

Straitlaced...that sounded negative somehow, boring. She wasn't boring—far from it. Dedicated, yes. And loving, passionate, clearheaded, for sure. It looked like the boys saw only the responsible older sister, and not the burden that she carried every day on those slender shoulders.

"Was she always like that?" Bryce asked.

"Oh, yeah." Randy shrugged. "Totally boring. All her friends moved away, and she stayed here instead. She should have done something, gone somewhere, but she was all about work and all that. I'm sure not sticking around here once I graduate."

Who knew what she might have done with fewer responsibilities weighing on her at home? When Randy got older he might appreciate it a little more when someone had made some hard choices in their youth. Randy loved his sister, but he didn't have the maturity to appreciate her sacrifices yet.

"You'll need some decent grades if you want to go to college," Bryce said. "Otherwise, you won't be leaving town, either."

"Yeah, I guess." Randy looked slightly worried, and he glanced in the direction of the high school. Bryce could only imagine the state of the kid's grades.

Seed planted, Bryce thought wryly.

"Well…" Bryce pushed himself back to his feet. "I guess I'd better get moving. Nice to see you around."

Randy's phone blipped and he picked it up, scanning the screen. "Do you like my sister, or something?" he asked, without looking up.

Was he so obvious? Instead, he said, "Who doesn't?"

Randy grinned and starting typing into his phone with two thumbs. He didn't look up as Bryce got back into the Loser Cruiser, and Bryce watched the kid for a moment, sorting through the details.

This was Lily's life—four boys who needed her more than they knew, and who took advantage of her every step of the way. She had enough demands piled on her that he wasn't even sure how she managed to keep that carefree smile on her face. At least he knew what was under it, now.

Lily didn't need any more burdens—including a guy messing with her emotions—and if last night's time with her family hadn't been enough to convince him that it was time to back off, then maybe this little chat with her brother could be the clincher. She had a life, a family and more responsibilities than she deserved, and he wasn't a part of that.

He couldn't offer what she wanted, so he needed to do her a favor and take a big step back.

That afternoon, Lily dropped the finished place cards and seating chart off at her aunt's house. Her aunt hadn't noticed that the list of Aaron's family members was missing. Hopefully, she never would, because Lily didn't believe in lying—not even little white ones—and she'd be forced to fess up her true feelings. The longer she could put that off the better.

After a couple of errands, she decided to treat herself with a small luxury—a caramel latte. She'd been craving one for a week now, and she'd been putting it off because she didn't believe in wasting pennies. She'd grown up pinching them, and even after giving her mother some extra money to help out with expenses, she still felt mildly guilty spending anything on herself. It would feel good to sit in one of the armchairs by the window and sip on a latte while Emily slept in her lap.

The baby had fallen asleep in the car, and Lily had discovered that morning that she'd grown just a bit heavier. It was significantly harder for Lily to carry the car seat in one hand when she went into stores. So instead of bringing the whole thing with her, she unbuckled Emily and carried her in her arms. It was nice to feel that warm little body propped against her shoulder. Emily wouldn't be this small for long, and she should probably appreciate how light she was to carry at this stage. If things went well—dare she hope it?— Lily would be able to look back on these days when Emily was a toddler or a preschooler and remember how tiny she used to be.

The coffee shop was located across the street from the hardware store at the corner of Main and Sycamore Drive. Lily nodded her thanks as an older gentleman in a white cowboy hat opened the door for her on his way out, and she stepped inside. It wasn't one of those fancy coffee shops you found on the corner of every city. There was a table with the newest copies of *Farming America*, *Ranch and Home* and *The Comfort Creek Gazette*. By the window overlooking the hardware store, there were several tables, and over by the door was a bookshelf packed with paperbacks. A handwritten sign read Lending Library. Honor System.

Lily needed to think…so much had been going on lately, and she wasn't even sure where to start getting her bearings. She'd been praying nonstop all morning, and while she tried to leave everything in God's capable hands, she'd always struggled with that. Doing something, fixing things—that was easier than trusting and waiting.

"What can I get for you?" the girl behind the counter asked.

Lily briefly considered a plain coffee with cream and sugar—her usual order—but she decided to satisfy that craving and placed her order. While her drink was being made, she glanced around the place and saw some older women she knew from church sitting in a cluster around three tables that they'd pushed together. They nodded politely, and she nodded back, her attention pulled back to the counter when she needed to pay. She adjusted Emily in her arms to pull out her wallet, and she left the change to go into the tip jar.

Behind her, the bell above the door tinkled, and she turned to see Bryce step inside. He saw her at the same time, and a smile broke over his face.

"Hi," he said. "Fancy seeing you here."

Her cup trembled in her hand, and he stepped forward to take it from her. His hand brushed hers as he took the cup from her fingers, and she gratefully adjusted Emily into a more comfortable position.

"Thanks." She shot him a smile, and they went to a table together. "Are you getting anything?"

"I'll be back," he said once she was settled, and he

went to give his order at the counter. The cluster of women followed Bryce with their eyes, and Lily stifled a smile. Not much happened in this town, and a man with Bryce's chiseled good looks was bound to draw attention. She could just overhear them talking about someone's grandson, from what she could make out. Apparently, his marriage was on the rocks.

"I saw your brother today," he said when he returned to the table with a mug of steaming coffee. "I think he's got a girlfriend."

"Which brother?" she asked with a wry smile.

"Randy."

"Oh, yes. Jen. She's a nice girl." Lily smiled wanly. "At sixteen, I don't think he's old enough to date, but Mom can't very well stop him." She paused, winced. Why was it that she kept blurting out all their family business? "Where did you see him?"

"At the corner store by the high school." He shrugged. "Nothing too interesting. I have to tell you, patrolling this town is like watching paint dry."

"I suppose that's a good thing," she said. "I don't think we want to be interesting in that way."

From the table of women, Lily could make out their conversation more clearly now. They were older women who didn't hear as well as they used to, so they also talked louder than they used to, too.

"…no, no, she's the illegitimate one."

"Oh, that's right. Well, I find it odd that she's the one that turned out. Those boys are headed nowhere good."

They were discussing her. Nice. She tried to keep a composed expression.

"Smoking and drinking." There was sharp disapproval in that voice. "And then their mother drags them off to church one Sunday a month and they sit in a row looking like they all need haircuts."

Lily felt the heat rise in her cheeks. They might be her elders, but she had half a mind to march over there and inform them that church was where her brothers belonged—and that they needed grace, not judgment. As for haircuts, those cost money, too, and talking behind their backs wouldn't help nearly so much as offering to pay for those haircuts. She knew what Comfort Creek thought of her family, so this wasn't exactly surprising, but being discussed so loudly was downright insulting.

In front of Bryce. That was the worst part of it—that Bryce would hear the worst.

Bryce glanced behind him toward the women, then leaned closer to Lily. "Who are they talking about?" he whispered.

"Me," she said with a tight smile. "I'm the illegitimate one, by the way."

There was no use hiding it. It was out there now. Bryce looked at her for a moment, then back at the women. They'd lowered their voices again. He wordlessly plucked Lily's cup out of her hand and strode to the counter.

"Could we get this to go, please?" he asked. The girl roused herself from the novel she'd been reading and complied, and then Bryce came back to the table.

"You drink your coffee, and I'll carry Piglet," he said brusquely. "Let's walk."

It wasn't a terrible idea, and as she passed the baby to Bryce, she saw the entire table of church ladies looking at them in open curiosity.

"By the way, ladies," Bryce said, turning toward

them with a warm smile on his face that looked just a hair too sweet to be sincere, "you should gossip more quietly. We heard all of that."

Faces blanched, and several of them turned their eyes quickly toward the table. One simply stared at Lily with regret written all over her face. She'd get some phone calls tonight from some apologetic gossips, she was sure.

Bryce led the way outside, and Lily followed. Out on the street, the sun was warm on her shoulders, and she took a sip of her latte.

"Thank you," she said with wry smile. "That was one way to do it."

"Better than simmering, right?" he asked with a cheerful grin. "Admit it, that felt good."

Lily laughed and shook her head. It actually had. On her own, she would have shoved all those angry feelings into the pit of her stomach and choked back her latte. She wouldn't have enjoyed a sip of it.

They ambled together down the sidewalk, past a stationery store, a meat shop, and then a bakery that poured the scent of fresh bread out into the street. Large planters of pink and purple flowers sat at each corner of the downtown sector of Comfort Creek, a blaze of color that Lily always looked forward to each spring. Across the street and past the stop sign and the flowers stood the police station in the shade of ancient elms.

"I thought your dad passed away in that accident," Bryce said after a moment.

"He was the only dad I ever knew," she said. "But not my biological father. My mom got pregnant with me at sixteen. She married my stepdad when I was five, and they started having the boys. But a place this size doesn't forget the pregnant sixteen-year-old."

"Yeah, apparently." He met her gaze with a sad smile. "Sorry about all that."

"What can you do?" she asked with a weak shrug.

He looked relaxed standing there in uniform with Emily dozing in his arms. Comfort Creek would never forget that Emily had arrived on a doorstep, but she'd never let Comfort Creek forget that she'd chosen this little girl with her whole heart. Emily needed a mom who could understand that kind of stigma.

"You have a lot of pressures here, don't you?" he said.

"Pressures?" She paused, considering the word. "Well, my family is here, and they rely on me."

"It seems like the police department relies on you, too," he said, looking down at Emily.

"I'm popular when they need something," she joked.

"Can I help?" he asked, blue eyes meeting hers. "I feel like I'm just one more burden for you."

"You aren't a burden." She shook her head. "You're my guest, Bryce."

His expression froze for a second, then he gave a quick nod. That hadn't been what she meant. Why was it that she could manage a professional distance at the very moment she didn't want one? He wasn't just a guest, but he also wasn't a problem to be solved, and she didn't know exactly how to categorize him.

"I didn't mean it quite like that," she said quietly. "You aren't a problem. You're—" she smiled uncertainly "—really, really nice."

Nice. That didn't cover what she meant, either, but

he seemed to hear what she meant in her voice, because he shot her a rueful smile.

"So are you, Miss Ellison." His voice was deep and warm, and as his eyes met hers, she saw tenderness in them. "Let me walk you back to your car."

Lily took a swig from her latte, and as they walked together back down Main Street, sauntering through the aroma of baking bread and the sweet scent of flowers, she realized that she didn't much care what Comfort Creek thought of her family.

There were some things a town would never forget, and there were other things that she'd never stop reminding them of, either. Emily would always be the baby left on a step, and Lily would always be the mother who loved her, if God would allow it. Her brothers might always be thought of as the troublemaking teens, but she'd always be the sister who defended them. There would be town opinion, and then there would be *her* opinion, and she'd strive every day to make sure that to a few very special people, her opinion would always matter more.

Chapter Twelve

The next morning, Bryce sat in the visitor's chair in Chief Morgan's office. The chief pushed a hot mug of coffee toward him. The room was relatively cool, and Bryce gave the chief a nod of thanks as he picked up his drink and took a sip.

"How have you been?" Chief Morgan asked.

"Fine, thanks."

"Using the notebook I gave you?"

Bryce patted his pocket, and his stomach sank. His front shirt pocket—where he'd been keeping the notebook—was empty. He grimaced.

"I forgot it this morning, but I've been using it. I promise you that."

The chief didn't look bothered, and he shrugged. "The point is that you've been using it."

Bryce felt a rush of relief. He'd hate to have the chief think he wasn't taking this seriously and send him to the binders for the rest of the week. Now, that would be punishment.

"So you were writing down the times that you felt like you were pretending to be something you weren't," the chief went on. "Writing it down is simply an exercise that makes you take note of it—makes you stop and think. So when did you find yourself faking it the most?"

He hated this. He hardly knew Chief Morgan, and talking about things this personal didn't come naturally to him. He was the bottling-up kind of guy, which apparently hadn't been working out for him that well. He shifted in his chair uncomfortably.

"I catch myself pretending to fit in here," he said.

"In what way?" the chief prodded.

Bryce frowned. "Slowing down, taking some interest in the locals…"

"And your interest in the locals…that isn't sincere?"

"No, it is." An image of Lily popped up in his mind, and his interest in her was very sincere. "But I'm a city cop, and I don't actually fit into things here. But I fake it. As I should, I suppose."

The chief nodded. "How about the minivan?"

"I truly loathe that vehicle, sir."

A grin broke over the other man's face and he laughed softly. "And when you drove it, did you act just a little bit tougher to compensate?"

Bryce considered for a moment, and perhaps he did. He was a big man, and he didn't normally need to pretend anything when it came to being intimidating with perps, but a minivan was demoralizing in a whole new way that he was sure he'd find funny later.

"That wasn't the biggest thing," Bryce said after a moment. "It was the baby."

"Oh, yeah?" Chief Morgan leaned forward. "How so?"

"Well, I'm terrible with kids, but Lily—" he shook his head, trying to gather his thoughts "—she doesn't get that. She just kept passing me the baby, and what was I supposed to do? I'm boarding at her B and B, and she's around and so is the baby... She can't exactly cook and all that with a baby in her arms—"

"What did you do?"

Bryce smiled wryly. "I held the baby."

"And pretended that you weren't quite so terrible with kids?" the chief prodded.

"Yeah, I guess so," Bryce said. "So what's the point of this, sir? To prove that we're all a bunch of fakes and liars?"

"In a way," the chief replied. "True strength is flexible. It bends and changes when pressure is applied. When something is too rigid, it breaks under pressure."

Rigid—like him, apparently. He'd certainly snapped when he decked Leroy. Bryce didn't say anything, just sat and waited.

"So back in Fort Collins," the chief said. "When you punched your coworker... What was it that you were faking then?"

Bryce's mind went back to the locker room with Leroy's leering face, and the laughter—it was the laughing that had gotten to him the most. Why he couldn't take it one more time, he'd never know, but a man's disappointment of a father wasn't joke material. Bryce had worked hard to distance himself from his old man, and he'd worked hard to prove that he was a better man, a better cop. That kind of stigma was hard to shake, if not impossible.

"Nothing anymore, sir," Bryce replied. "He'd poked a sore spot. I snapped. If I'd been faking anything, I'd have just walked away, pretended it didn't get to me. Nothing was more honest than that punch, sir."

"And what were you faking until you snapped?"

Bryce considered a moment, and the truth of the matter burned up the inside of him like rising bile. "I was pretending I was nothing like my father."

The chief nodded slowly. "The truth can flex and spring back when pressure is applied to it. It can adjust to new situations. A lie can't. It just snaps."

Bryce was silent. He'd spent his entire life pretending he was nothing like his father, trying to prove his mother's worries wrong. He'd accepted that he was like his dad when it came to children, but maybe it went deeper than that. Maybe it was worse than he'd thought.

"So you're saying I'm just like him?" Bryce asked after a moment.

"It isn't what I think," the chief replied. "It's what you think. And if you can't embrace yourself, flaws and all, you'll just keep snapping."

"I'm not like him," Bryce said, his voice a growl. "He's my father, but I'm not his clone."

"True."

"So that was the point of all of this—to convince me that the apple didn't fall so far from the tree?" Bryce put a cap on the anger simmering deep within him, but it was still there. "With all due respect, sir, I think I prefer the binders."

He'd made a mistake—one mistake in the course of his career so far. He'd lashed out in a juvenile way, but that didn't give this relative stranger a right to judge his ability to be a cop. He'd learned from his error, and he wouldn't be snapping like that again. He was perfectly capable of controlling himself, and he'd do that. This was a job, and they didn't have a right to his most personal hang-ups and feelings.

"If you want," the chief said with a shrug. "But I was going to send you back out on patrol."

"For what, exactly?" Bryce retorted.

"You're a good cop, Bryce."

He *was* a good cop. He knew that about himself. He cared about those streets, about keeping families safe and stopping crime. He cared about protecting the innocent, and making sure that no one got taken advantage of. He even cared about the riffraff he arrested—because they were people, too, and generally, they were people with problems bigger than they could handle. He was good at this job, and one mistake in a locker room didn't change how much he cared about the community he protected.

But he was here to prove that. One mistake had come with consequences, and he couldn't just walk away from those. His father had walked away from too many things in his life, starting with his family and ending with his career. Bryce wouldn't do that—he'd stand his ground.

"So what is your advice, then, sir?" he asked after a moment.

"Stop pretending," Chief Morgan replied. "Live in the light. Be who you are with integrity and honesty. It frees up all the energy you spend trying to hide things for something more useful—like your family, or your career."

He didn't have a family who needed his attention, but he got what the chief was trying to say. Maybe it was time to accept facts. He was the son of Richard Camden—for all the good things and the challenges it posed. He could fight it, and he could fake it, but nothing would change the simple facts.

"Thanks, sir," Bryce said.

"Now, I'll sign off on your sensitivity training after your shift on Saturday. Then you'll be free to head back. Have a good day on patrol." Chief Morgan stood up and shook Bryce's hand. "Unless you were serious about those binders…"

Bryce laughed softly. "I'll take patrol, sir."

He had a lot to think about, and driving through the streets of Comfort Creek was the perfect way to do that. Nothing happened here anyway.

Lily came up the stairs with a pile of clean sheets in one arm, topped by the baby monitor and a wrapped chocolate for the pillow. In the other hand, she carried a vase with fresh daisies. She'd never liked the smell of daisies, but they were cheerful, and she thought they would go nicely on the bedside table.

Her first guest would enjoy the best she had to offer. Bryce. Bryce would enjoy all of this, because he was her guest, and because she wanted him to feel comfortable for his last few days here before she had to say goodbye.

That thought had been weighing on her all morning—their goodbye was coming. Bryce wasn't here for long, and by the weekend, when Aunt Clarisse was getting married for better for worse, Bryce would be on his way back to his life in the city.

Lily pushed open the bedroom door, and she was met with the same cleanliness she saw every morning when she came in to change the bed and do a quick dust. His suitcase was zipped shut, sitting on the seat of the chair, and the bed was already made with military precision.

She deposited the sheets and vase on the top of the dresser, but as she turned toward the room, something fell to floor behind her. It was a small notebook—she must have knocked it off. She bent to pick it up, and it had fallen open to the first page.

I shouldn't read this, she told herself, but her eyes were already skimming over the words.

The first thing was written in a different hand, and it read: *Write down every time you pretend to be something you are not*. This was the notebook Bryce had mentioned—that sensitivity training he'd come to Comfort Creek to complete. It wasn't right to pry into something so personal, but somehow she couldn't stop her eyes from absorbing the words on the page written in Bryce's strong, confident handwriting.

Pretending I don't notice how pretty she is. Doris Day. Grace Kelly. She's like an old-fashioned movie star, and I half expect her to dance and sing.

Was Bryce referring to her? She blushed at that. She liked to think it was her, but truthfully, it could be anyone. Maybe he'd seen a woman in the street who inspired that.

Pretending I don't smell that diaper. Wow—that's pungent!

That was most definitely Emily. She smiled at that.

Pretending I'm comfortable holding the baby. I'm not good at this. Keep pretending it's no big deal.

Actually, he didn't convince her that holding Emily was no big deal—at least he hadn't until recently. For the first few days he turned stiff as wood every time she passed him the baby to hold. It was endearing that he thought he'd hidden that, though.

Pretending I fit in here.

Pretending I have something important to do while I drive around these silent streets.

Pretending I'm not being disciplined for something so stupid.

She turned the page, and the handwriting continued.

Pretending I care about lawn fertilizer. I don't. I really, really don't.

She chuckled at that one, and her eyes went down to the bottom of the opposite page.

Sitting with Piglet in my arms, pretending I could do this—be a dad one day. I can't, though. This one only hurts me.

Lily shut the book and placed it on the bedside table, her heart pounding. He was wrong there—that one didn't only hurt him. Of course, she had told herself not to expect more, not to hope for more, but reading his own script in the confession that he could never be a father—that had unexpectedly stabbed her. Had she really been hoping that Bryce would be a part of this picture with her?

She didn't have a right to read those pages. She knew that, and she felt a pang of guilt for having read as much as she had. She grabbed the blanket and pulled it off the bed, then stripped the sheets and tossed them with more force than necessary into a pile by the door.

Clean sheets. She'd vowed that every night her guests would sleep on clean sheets—no matter how long their stay with her.

After her stepfather died, Lily remembered one weekend morning when they were stripping the sheets off all the beds to do laundry. Her mother looked wan and worried. The landlord had been by to collect the rent again. Except they didn't have the rent to give, and he'd blustered and shamed them a little before stomping off again, and Iris had said, "Let's go change the sheets."

It had seemed like such a strange reaction to the landlord's threats of eviction and eventual homelessness, but Lily had done what her mother had asked, and they went about stripping the beds and remaking them with fresh, clean-smelling sheets.

"Mom, the sheets don't matter!" Lily had finally wailed. "He's going to kick us out!"

"The sheets do matter," her mother said, holding back tears. "Our life might be falling apart, but that's no excuse to look shabby. *We* are not shabby."

Shaking out the fresh bottom sheet over the mattress, Lily couldn't help but remember her mother's stubborn persistence when it came to appearances. A fresh bed mattered. A clean floor, a wiped counter— they mattered deeply, because to her mother they reflected on more than circumstances; they announced who they were. And the Ellisons were not shabby people.

She tucked the sheet in snugly, then flapped out the top sheet. Making a bed was something she enjoyed because she could make something comfortable and attractive so easily. Fresh, crisp sheets felt wonderful when a tired body slipped between them at night, and all those difficult years when she was growing up, she'd always crawled between smooth, sweet-smelling sheets each night.

"You are worth clean sheets, Lily," her mother had told her. "Don't let those things slip, because it's too easy to forget that you matter if you let your home become sloppy."

This had been her mother's way of showing them that they were more than their financial situation— more than the stigma that dogged them in this town. And no matter what she was struggling with, Lily had always found comfort in a well-made bed.

She placed the chocolate on the pillow when she was finished, and then brought the fresh vase of flowers to the bedside table. The little book lay where she'd left it, and she looked at it for a minute or two, staring down at the closed cover.

It was a book of confessions, the truth beneath the veneer. She could fall in love with this flawed man so very easily, but she could not change him. He didn't want to be a father—he couldn't find that piece inside of himself that would make it possible—and that wouldn't change just because she hoped things could be different.

I still want Emily, she prayed silently. *I know I'd raise her alone, Lord, and I know I've been picturing Bryce as part of all of this, but I still want to raise her.*

She shouldn't have read his private book, but perhaps it was better to have seen the truth. It was silly to hope for something that wouldn't happen, even if that hope was in a very illogical, fantasy-based place in her heart where she'd stowed away the princess castles and knights on chargers. She knew better than this. Life had taught her better than this.

She picked up the baby monitor, then bent and gathered up the sheets to take down to the laundry. Life had a way of teaching all sorts of painful and difficult lessons, like to be skeptical of any story that began with *Once upon a time…*

But God had also taught her lessons over the years,

like to hold on when it looked as though your family was about to be homeless, because He'd provide a wealthy family in the church to slip an envelope of money to her mother one Sunday, enough to pay all the rent owed. He'd taught her that comfort could be found in the least expected places, like in the arms of an elderly woman she hardly knew who hugged her at her stepfather's funeral and whispered, "I lost my daddy, too, when I was your age. Things will get better..." God had taught her to hold on and to hope, and in her devotions when she read the old stories of Isaac and Rebecca, Boaz and Ruth, Joseph and Mary, He'd reminded her with every beat of her heart that stories didn't have to begin with *Once upon a time* in order to have a soul mate at the end.

But sometimes, the man who inexplicably filled your mind wasn't the one God had in His.

Chapter Thirteen

Bryce didn't go back to Lily's house after his shift. Instead, he went out to eat at a little diner along the highway where he had a rather tough steak with a side of mashed potatoes and he stared down into his coffee mug for a long time thinking about his discussion with the chief that morning.

A lot of what he'd said hit home. Bryce was who he was. He could pretend that he didn't come from such demoralizing pedigree, but there was no use in that. As long as he tried to hide who he was, the more power he gave to guys like Leroy Higgins.

I'm a good cop.

So far, it was the only thing he was really good at, and if he could follow the chief's advice and embrace who he was, maybe he could avoid some of his father's career pitfalls, too.

He'd stayed away from Lily today purposely because he knew that when he got around her, he started thinking about things he couldn't have. He was falling for her, against all his better judgment, and that would only set him back. It wasn't wise to wish for things you'd never have—he'd learned that growing up without a dad. His father would make his annual Christmas guilt offering—generally toys that were too young for him—and then disappear again. Wishing that his dad would come back didn't make it happen, and he'd steeled himself early to the things he knew better than to pine for.

And that was his plan for his feelings for Lily. He knew how to shut himself down. He knew how to turn off his feelings when he needed to, so why wasn't it working when he thought about her?

Lord, just turn off these feelings, he prayed. *I know I can't have this life—I have nothing to offer a woman like her. So please, just shut it down for me. I can't seem to do it on my own this time.*

After his dinner, he went back to the Loser Cruiser and sat staring at his father's email on his cell phone. This whole mess had been surrounding his old man, and he wondered if it was time to have another talk with his dad—an adult one.

He wasn't going to be free of this until he did—he knew that much. He closed his eyes for a moment, saying a silent prayer for whatever was about to happen, and dialed the number. It rang four times before his father picked up.

"Yeah?" He sounded like he'd been sleeping.

"Hi. It's Bryce."

"Oh..." Some rustling, a cleared throat. "Hey, Bryce. You got my email, then?"

"Yeah, I got it." Bryce leaned his head back against the headrest. "Did I wake you up or something?"

"Sort of. Don't worry about it. So how are things in sensitivity training?"

"Not too bad," Bryce said.

"I know the guy running it," his father said. "Back when I did my bouts of sensitivity training, it was all book work in the basement of the Fort Collins station. Looks like you're getting the royal treatment."

"He said you were partners back in the day," Bryce said, then cleared his throat. "So why did you email?"

"You're my kid."

He was his kid... Not that it seemed to matter all those years when he was actually a child.

"It's been a long time," Bryce said, his words loaded with meaning.

"I know. I thought you could use some moral support about now."

"I could have used it on my birthdays, too," Bryce countered. "I could have used it at my high school graduation."

"Hey, I showed up when it mattered." Anger edged his father's tone. "I pulled you out of trouble. So don't go saying I didn't do anything for you—"

That was the pattern, though—his father showed up to rescue him when Bryce had gotten into trouble. Not beforehand, and not in time to avoid it...just in time to try to pick up the pieces with him.

"But why now?" Bryce pressed. "Why not at any other time, Dad?"

"Because you needed me this time." His father heaved a sigh. "Bryce, your mom is a good woman, and she could handle all the other stuff. She did birthdays and homework and kept on top of you with your grades...but this is the stuff she wouldn't understand. This my arena."

"The mess-ups," Bryce clarified.

"The tough stuff." There was silence for several beats. "Look, I've been there. I've gotten in trouble and been embarrassed. I've gotten mixed up in stuff that got away from me. I understand this part, and I'm pretty sure you need someone who does."

And as bitter as that was, his dad had a point. If anyone knew what it was like to hit rock bottom, it was his old man. He hadn't talked any of this through with his mother because his dad was right—she wasn't the one to understand what he was going through.

"So what's your advice?" Bryce asked.

"Not sure," his father replied. "Just keep it under control. Don't let your temper get the better of you."

Sage words. Bryce pulled his hand through his hair. "Great. Got it."

"Look," his father said. "I know it's been hard for you since I left the force, and all that. I'm just sorry that it had to be that way. It wasn't my plan. Just wanted you to know that."

Of course it hadn't been his father's plan to end up in disgrace, but the apology was nice, regardless.

"Yeah, I know..."

"You didn't mean to end up in Comfort Creek, either," his father went on. "These things happen. I get it."

"No." Bryce shook his head, the old anger bubbling up once more. "These things don't just happen, Dad. I didn't just accidentally punch another officer."

"So what happened?" his father asked.

"I was defending you!" His voice broke as the words came out. It was like he'd been a kid on the playground all over again, defending a father who was never around. *He does too love me! He's just super busy, so shut up already!*

"You just couldn't do it," Bryce went on. "You told me that a few times—you just couldn't be the husband and father we needed. I actually get that now that I'm an adult—except I was already there, Dad! This wasn't about you choosing to have kids or not. You had one."

"I know," his father said. "What do you want from me? To say I'm sorry again?"

What did he want? Bryce didn't even know. He wanted to rewind the last twenty-odd years and actually have a relationship with his father. He wanted his school yard tales about his dad to be true, not made-up stories that gave him a perverse sort of comfort. He wanted the words "You're just like your dad" to be a compliment, not ominous foreshadowing of his future.

"I want to get together once a month for a meal," Bryce said after a moment.

"What?" His father sounded hesitant, nervous.

"You asked what I wanted," Bryce said. "I want to get together at a greasy spoon burger joint, eat our body weight in beef, and talk. That's what I want."

"Okay."

It was Bryce's turn to hesitate. "You've promised stuff before, Dad. You've said you'd be there for how many baseball games, how many class plays? You said you'd do a lot, but I'm not a kid anymore, and I'm not asking for you to just say something nice to make me go away. If you probably won't do this, then tell me now."

"No, no… I could do that. Once a month, you say?"

"Once a month. We don't have to talk about anything deep, but I want some kind of relationship, because what we've got right now doesn't count for much."

"I can do that," his dad replied. "I like burgers, too."

It was a deal. Sort of. Bryce would have to see what came of it, because he'd had an entire life of disappointments where his dad was concerned. But maybe, if they could start sitting down together and talking about sports and the weather during the good times, they could actually develop some sort of relationship. Maybe he could be one of those men who said things like, "Sorry, can't make it. I'm getting together with my dad this weekend. Maybe next time." Simple things like bailing on plans with buddies for his dad—funny how small his fantasy life was.

"Okay, well…" Bryce cleared his throat. "I'll give you a call when I'm done here in Comfort Creek, and we can set something up."

After an awkward goodbye, Bryce hung up and stared at his phone in his hand. He was afraid to hope, but hope had sparked up inside him anyway.

God…

He had no idea what to pray for—for his father to pick up the phone when he called next, or for Bryce to tamp out the hope now—but the connection to his heavenly father helped, because his earthly dad was a piece of work.

When he pulled into the drive at the house and turned off the engine, he could hear Piglet's cry before he even got to the door. The sun had set already, and the sky was that mauve color, just between daylight and night darkness, a couple of the brightest stars piercing through. The baby's cry was long and pitiful—not a wail of rage. It was strange that he could tell that from the front step, but he could. He looked back toward the quiet road behind him, and he briefly considering getting back into his truck—that's what the old Bryce would have done—but he couldn't quite make himself do it.

Maybe he could calm the kid down. She liked him, after all. When he opened the door, he looked cautiously around. Lily stood in the middle of the sitting room. She was surrounded by baby paraphernalia—bottles, pacifiers, blankets, rags, even an open bottle of some sort of diaper cream—and her face looked pale and tired.

"Hi," she said, raising her voice above the baby's cry. Piglet was in her arms, her little face red with the exertion of her cries. "How was your day?"

It was almost a ridiculous question, because looking at Lily, she probably didn't care a whole lot how his day had gone. Nor should it matter. It had all fallen apart here, apparently.

Bryce chuckled. "Want me to try?"

Lily gratefully handed Piglet over. The baby didn't go smoothly, and she writhed and stretched. He managed to get her positioned against his chest, and he patted her back gently and looked into her tiny face.

"Hey, there, kiddo," he said softly. "What's all this about?"

Piglet paused in her cries for a moment at the sound of his voice, teary eyes blinking tiredly, then she picked up again with new fervor. It looked like he'd lost the touch, which was just as well. Maybe Piglet was getting better taste in men already.

"I have an idea," Lily said, disappearing into the kitchen for a moment, and then returning with the car seat. "I'm taking her for a drive. It worked wonders with my little brothers when they got worked up like this. If you'd just hold her for a minute, I can get this set up—"

"Let me." Bryce's bravado had less to do with a desire to manhandle a car seat than it was a very strong wish to hand the wailing baby back to Lily. In a way, it felt good to be reassured that his stretch of baby whispering seemed to be finished. It was better this way—clearer.

He marched out and opened the back door of his truck. He knew how to put these in from safety days put on by the station in Fort Collins where officers helped parents get their children's car seats installed properly, and it didn't take him long.

"Let's go!" he called, and Lily came out with a diaper bag in one hand and the wailing Piglet up on her shoulder. Lily had slipped some flip-flops on her feet, and she was the least put together he'd seen her yet, but she still managed to look endearing.

"Are you driving?" she asked, and he thought he heard some relief in her voice. He didn't know how long she'd spent trying to soothe the baby, but it had taken a toll on her.

"Yeah, I'll drive," he said. He wouldn't be able to rest in the empty house anyway. He had too much roiling around in his head.

Within five minutes they were cruising down the gravel road toward the highway, the rumble of his truck's engine partially drowning out Piglet's cries, but she was losing steam, and that was something. The dirt road crunched beneath his tires at a satisfying rate, and he listened to the pummel of tiny rocks smacking the side of his truck. The evergreen trees rose dark and protective along the side of the road, and the rising moon cast a silvery glow over the scene.

"I think it's working," Lily said, looking back into the car seat. She reached back to arrange something, and the sound of pacifier sucking suddenly filled the vehicle.

"Nice," Bryce said with a half smile.

Lily heaved a sigh and leaned her head back. "Wow. She just wouldn't calm down. Thanks for driving."

"Not a problem." Frankly, it felt good to solve something, and they fell into silence, listening to the sound of Piglet's pacifier getting slower and slower. She was falling asleep.

"You must have been busy today…" Lily glanced toward him, then away. She was commenting on him staying away this long. It shouldn't matter what he did with his time, but somehow they'd fallen into a kind of dependence on each other.

"Yeah." He wasn't sure how to explain that one to her. "I thought it would be better."

"Better?" She frowned. "Why?"

He smiled wryly, but didn't answer. No good could come from admitting to what he'd been feeling lately. He slowed and made the turn onto the highway.

"I checked in with the chief about finding the ID Aaron used to get a Colorado driver's license, and we're still waiting," Bryce said after a moment.

"Is there any way to hurry it up?" Lily asked. "The wedding is tomorrow night. Or are we too late already?"

He understood her urgency. This rushed wedding

wasn't wise on Clarisse's part, and he knew that Lily only wanted to protect her emotionally vulnerable aunt. So did he, for that matter. If Aaron Bay turned out to be a con man, he'd personally make sure the charges stuck.

"I'll see what I can do," he replied. "Look, Lily, even if it takes longer—"

"She'll be on her honeymoon—in Europe." Lily's earnest gaze met his. "Off American soil, Bryce. That worries me. If Aaron has anything to hide, we need to find it soon!"

"I'm on it." He meant that. They drove on in silence for a little while, both of them in their own thoughts.

Lily nodded, then slipped off her flip-flops and pulled her feet up underneath her. She was petite, and she fit into the seat very comfortably that way. The scent of her soft perfume wafted over to him.

"You're leaving tomorrow, aren't you?" she asked.

"I have one more shift at the station, and then I'm free to go," he clarified.

"Will you come to the wedding?" she asked.

He smiled sadly. "Do you really want me to?"

"Of course." She shot him a smile. "You could be my plus one."

Was it a good idea? Truthfully, he didn't want to leave, and it was an excuse to stay one day longer. But dragging this out wouldn't make it any easier, either.

"I'll see what I can do." He didn't want to promise anything—not while he was trying to hold himself in check. One more shift, and he was done with Comfort Creek; he could go back to Fort Collins and put this whole disciplinary action behind him. One more shift...

"The next left is Wichita Lake," Lily said. "It's pretty out there."

Bryce signaled a turn. "The longer we drive, the longer she sleeps."

It was strangely comforting to be driving with Lily. Wichita Lake. Why not?

"You know, maybe I could come back out this way for a weekend or something," Bryce said. "Comfort Creek is growing on me."

"Is it?" Lily shot him a smile. "We do have the lake… I should have pointed it out earlier."

"That's okay. I was supposed to be suffering anyway," he joked.

Lily laughed softly. "Was it really so miserable?"

He'd been in a comfortable room with fresh flowers that kept appearing every day, a chocolate on his pillow and sheets that smelled like they were line-dried. It wasn't exactly Alcatraz. But besides the homey comforts of the bed-and-breakfast, he'd had her…and she'd been this oddly talkative, humorous, insightful woman who kept drawing him back, even managing to get him to hold a baby because she never seemed to fully grasp that he wasn't good with kids. That smile of hers just seemed to empty his head of every great excuse he had…

The trees suddenly parted, and a dirt parking lot opened up before them with a couple of public buildings to the side. The lake was straight ahead—a rocky beach, then the glitter of moonlight on water. Bryce parked, but he kept the motor running.

"Miserable?" he said, casting her a gentle smile. "Nah, I'm surviving."

And in some ways, that was what he was just barely doing.

* * *

Lily turned her gaze toward the lake, her heart full of emotions she'd been trying to hold down the last week. She shouldn't be getting used to this, yet somehow she'd been relying on Bryce in ways she had no right to. He wasn't hers... He didn't belong here. He was a paying guest, and she'd somehow crossed that line.

"Do you still long for a bit of freedom?" Bryce asked quietly.

"Always." She laughed softly. "It's just a fantasy. I think we all know where reality ends and fantasy begins."

"When I saw Randy the other day, he mentioned that all your friends moved away."

"They did." She could still remember how empty and lonely that fall was when her high school friends were gone and she'd been left in Comfort Creek without them. That summer, she'd had to face that her adult life had officially begun. She'd always had responsibilities, but now she had them without a small but loyal group of friends she saw on a daily basis. It was harder somehow, more real.

"You could leave here," Bryce said, and she caught a tremor of hope in his voice.

"Where would I go?" she asked.

"Ever been to Fort Collins?" A small smile tugged at his lips. "It's a nice place."

Lily sighed. That wasn't a possibility. The responsibilities that tied her down at the end of high school hadn't gone anywhere.

"I have a life here, Bryce," she said. "I can't just move to a new city on my own—"

"You'd have me." He reached out and took her hand in his, his calloused fingers moving over her skin in slow circles. "It might be nice to have a life that's yours for a change."

She'd have him. That was more tempting than maybe he even realized, but her wishes didn't change facts.

"I just started a business. I can't simply walk away—" Anger was rising up inside her—an effective cap for that welling sadness. "I've put everything into this—worked so hard. You have no idea!"

"Are you mad at me?" he asked hesitantly.

Lily struggled to keep her voice down, not wanting to wake Emily in the backseat. She unbuckled her seat belt and wordlessly got out of the truck. Bryce got out, too, and Lily paced toward the rocky beach, then turned back.

"It's probably my fault, Bryce," she said. "I get that. I haven't been professional at all, and I'm sure I gave you mixed messages, and—"

"You said you wanted some freedom," Bryce said. "And the thing is, I can't stop thinking about you."

The emotion in his words flooded out her anger, leaving her trembling with uncertain feelings.

"Why?" she demanded. "I'm not your problem. Neither are my brothers."

"My problem?" He shook his head, his eyes flashing in rising anger of his own. "You aren't my problem, and I'm not trying to fix you. You don't need me for that. You're…amazing. You're sweet and funny, and for crying out loud, do you have any idea how gorgeous you are? I don't want to feel like this—you complicate everything, Lily! I had it all under control. You might not realize it to look at me, but I did! I knew what I needed, I knew what I wanted, and I knew exactly what path I was going to take to get there, and then you came along."

"Sorry about that." She smiled sadly. "I'm terrible at professional boundaries."

"Yeah, you really are." He stepped closer, blue eyes boring down into hers. He touched her cheek with the back of a finger, and his lips were so close to hers that she could feel his breath. "I'm not much better at the moment. I don't know if I could be enough—"

Lily blinked, then swallowed hard. Had she heard him properly?

"You…"

Bryce dipped his head down and caught her lips in a kiss. It was tender, sweet and filled with longing. She twined her arms around his neck, and he slipped his around her waist, tugging her closer. All of those feelings she'd been trying to hold back came with the force of a flood, and she wished so deeply that she could give in to this. When he finally pulled back, she felt breathless.

"Do you feel it?" he asked, misery written all over his face.

She nodded. "Yeah…" she whispered.

"If we wanted to, we could find a way to make this work," he pressed.

She'd asked God for a chance to be Emily's mother, and she'd promised Him that she'd always put Emily first. If she chose Bryce, she'd be turning her back on that little girl. Bryce had been very clear about where he stood about being a dad, and he'd already backed out of one wedding because a woman thought she could change him.

"I can't." Lily pushed herself away from him and walked off a few steps, her heart hammering. Bryce didn't say anything, and when she turned back toward him, the big cop was staring at her with unnamable emotions battling over his face.

"Why?"

"We want different things out of life, Bryce."

"Because you want kids." His voice was tight with restrained emotion. "And I can't offer that. I can just offer…me."

He was offering all that he could—his very heart. He was putting it there for her to consider, and she wished that he wouldn't, because it only made this harder. If things were different, she might have been tempted to reevaluate what she wanted in her future. But it wasn't about some future children she might want to have. It wasn't about one day starting a family. It was about a baby girl who was already here, whom Lily already loved.

"Because I want to keep Emily."

Bryce froze, then nodded slowly. "I thought you were temporary foster care…"

"I was. I am. I'm looking into it. I don't want to give her up, Bryce. I know I have all sorts of responsibilities here. I have my brothers, my mom, my aunt… I have my business. My *life* is here. But it's not only that—it's Emily. I can't just give up, not without at least trying—"

"Yeah." He nodded quickly. "I get it."

They stood in miserable silence, the waves lapping gently at the rocky shore. Lily looked over the water at a flock of ducks floating peacefully in the moonlight. She'd told God that she was willing to put Emily first for the rest of her life, and she was recognizing now what a big promise she'd made. Tears welled up in her eyes. She didn't want Bryce to go, and she didn't want to give up Emily. Right now, her only comfort was in her heavenly father who was the only one who truly understood how deeply her heart ached.

"You could stay..." she said quietly.

"I'm not cut out for fatherhood," he said woodenly. "I know that."

And she knew it, too, from his little book of confessions. This was Bryce—and he knew what he could offer. Fatherhood wasn't on the table.

"I wish you could—" She couldn't finish that thought aloud. "You've been honest with me from the start...but I can't give her up."

"And you shouldn't." He nodded quickly.

"I'm going to miss you, Bryce." Her voice was choked with tears.

"Me, too." He raked a hand through his dark hair. "If you ever need anything, though..."

She shook her head. "No. I've got to do this on my own."

And she meant it. It had been her mistake to start relying on him to begin with. If she'd stayed a little more determined to do this on her own, she might not have fallen for the dark, rugged officer to begin with. She didn't need support, or rescuing, or to be set free from her responsibilities. She needed—

Tears squeezed between her lids, and she dashed them off her cheeks with the back of her hand. She needed time. Because nothing else was going to heal her heart.

Chapter Fourteen

That night, Bryce didn't sleep easily. He lay awake a long time, and when he finally drifted off, he was plagued by disjointed dreams. He woke up and turned on the lamp. He'd read his Bible—it was a better option than tossing and turning for the next few hours.

Early that morning, he got a text from his buddy in the FBI. If Bryce could make it to the records department in Fort Collins, his friend could get him inside. It was after hours, a Saturday, and his friend was going to be there for another case, but if Bryce wanted to tag along, maybe he could get that info he'd been waiting on...

It was tempting, but if Bryce wanted to get a signature for his sensitivity training here in Comfort Creek, then he needed to complete one more shift of patrol. If there was nothing to find, and Aaron Bay was just a guy with a weird paper trail, then he'd have wasted this time here in Comfort Creek, and would get another mark against him on his record for disobeying orders. This was his career he was playing with—his future.

When Bryce came downstairs, Lily had a delicious

breakfast spread on the table—fluffy pancakes, crisp bacon and a bowl of fresh strawberries to go on top. He hadn't been sure he'd even see her this morning after everything they'd said last night. He'd been half-afraid that she'd be embarrassed and not want to face him again, but when he went to the kitchen in his uniform, she was cutting fruit with her back to him, an apron tied around her slim waist.

"Morning," he said quietly.

She turned and attempted to smile. "Good morning. I have breakfast ready." Her eyes were red as if she'd been crying, and he paused—

Were those tears because of him? He could have stayed strong, done his time and walked away from this town, but he knew even now that he wouldn't have been able to do that. He had to tell her what he felt, or it would have eaten him alive. But if he'd caused her pain—

"Look, Lily—" he began. "Maybe I should have kept all that to myself last night…"

"No," she said with a shake of her head. "It's okay. I'm glad you said something."

"You haven't changed your mind, have you?" he asked hopefully.

She was silent for moment, and when she spoke, her voice was tight with emotion. "I told God I wanted to raise Emily, and that if He would let me, that I'd always put her first. I hadn't realized how much I'd have to give up."

The sadness in her eyes was so deep that he longed to wrap his arms around her and kiss her pain away, but he wouldn't. He couldn't. He wasn't her answer, and he had to accept that.

"I always suspected that in order to stand by my convictions—" he swallowed "—in order to do the right thing and stay away from fatherhood, that I'd be giving up more than I ever knew, too."

"So I'm not alone in that," she said with a sad smile.

"Not at all, beautiful. Not at all."

Lily wiped her hands on a towel and crossed the kitchen. She didn't stop—she came right into his arms and leaned the side of her face against his chest, wrapping her arms around his waist. He closed his arms around her and pressed his lips to the top of her silky golden hair. She smelled of fragrant shampoo and pancakes, and she felt so good in his arms that a lump rose in his throat.

"I'm sorry," he whispered.

"Me, too." She pulled away and brushed a tear from her cheek. "I just needed to do that." She forced a smile to her face and nodded toward the table. "Breakfast is served."

As if he could swallow a bite.

"The wedding is today?" he said. "Clarisse is still set?"

She nodded. "Unless you can find something before sunset. That's when the wedding is happening on the church lawn. A sunset wedding…so romantic—or it would be, if I weren't scared to death that she's going to be taken advantage of."

"I have a day," he said. "I can't promise anything, but I'll do my best."

It was Saturday, though, and very little could be done with emails or phone calls. He'd spent a week doing all the footwork he could from here, and not getting much back.

"Will you?" she asked uncertainly. "Still?"

Did she think he was so fickle that he'd walk out on her when she needed him most, just because it couldn't work between them? He wasn't that kind of man—but this wasn't virtue, this was the only way to keep his aching heart from breaking in his chest. He had to *do* something. With all the worries she shouldered, if he could help her with one of them, he would. Maybe this could be his parting gift.

"Hey—" His voice dropped low and deep, and he caught her eye and held it. "Whether we can be together or not, whether you want me or not, it doesn't change who I am. I said I'd look into Aaron Bay, and I'm finishing the job."

Tears welled in her eyes. "Thank you."

He wasn't supposed to leave town, but he knew what he had to do…even if it meant that he wouldn't get that signature…even if it meant being suspended for insubordination. He could join the Camden legacy.

Bryce looked at his watch, then pulled out his phone and typed a text back to his friend in the FBI.

On my way. I'll be there in two hours.

Clarisse stood in front of her bedroom mirror, smoothing the front of her wedding dress. Lily watched as she leaned closer to check her lipstick again, then slipped her feet into the ivory satin shoes, giving her another inch of height.

Emily lay in Lily's arms sleeping peacefully. She was so little—but she was getting bigger. She was heavier now than she used to be, and Lily felt a source of pride in watching the baby girl thrive. She was pudgier now, too.

Aunt Clarisse pressed her lips together to even her lipstick, then dabbed at it with a tissue.

"You look beautiful, Auntie," she said with a smile. "Stop fussing."

"You look more nervous than I am," Clarisse said, shooting Lily a smile over her shoulder.

"Do I?" What was Lily supposed to say to that? This was the evening of Clarisse's wedding, and Lily hadn't heard anything from Bryce. She'd tried calling his cell phone a few times, but it went straight to voice mail. Lily had no more information to go on than she'd had that morning, and perhaps it was better to just support her aunt and pray for the best. This was out of her hands now.

"Are you sure about this, Auntie?" Lily asked after a moment.

"Positive." Clarisse turned from the mirror and sank onto the side of the bed next to Lily. "You'll have to trust me on this one, dear."

And she would. There was no way around it.

"I'm more concerned about you," her aunt said quietly.

"Me?" Lily stretched her legs out in front of her. She wore a tea-length dress of pale violet to complement her aunt's, and she smoothed a hand over the silk. "Why?"

"Because you love him."

Lily's eyes misted. She hadn't said anything about loving Bryce —how had her aunt figured it out? She cuddled Emily just a little closer. "What do you mean?"

"Oh, don't be silly," Clarisse said sympathetically. "Aaron and I could see it plain as day. The two of you were in love with each other. But you look miserable, and Bryce is nowhere to be seen. So yes, I'm more concerned about you."

Lily fell silent. It wasn't something they could fix. This wasn't some misunderstanding or hurt feelings—this was the kind of roadblock that couldn't be overcome. They wanted different things. It was supposed to be straightforward and logical. She was supposed to be able to move on. She'd made her choice, and she'd chosen Emily.

"You take too much onto yourself," her aunt said. "If you ran off and married Bryce, you'd have a bit of freedom, and you deserve that. Life won't fall apart here."

"That's what Bryce said last night," she admitted sadly…well, except for the marrying part. But it wasn't only about her responsibilities here in town; it was about Emily, too.

"Did he?" Clarisse reached over and took her hand. "You're twenty-five, not fifty. I worry about how much you try to deal with alone."

"I want to raise Emily," Lily said. "I know it's a big job, and I know I already have a business to run, but I can't just give her up, and Emily deserves someone who loves her like that."

"She does," Clarisse said. "And why doesn't Bryce fit into this?"

"He doesn't want kids." The lump in her throat choked off her voice. She swallowed hard. "He's been very clear about it from the start. He knows his mind on this, and it isn't about convincing him otherwise. I know what I have to do, but it isn't easy…"

Clarisse shifted on the bed to face Lily, and she

fixed her with a serious look. "You have to choose between them, then."

"Yes." Lily wished that her chin hadn't trembled when she said it.

"Oh, Lily…" Her aunt put a hand over hers, sympathy welling in her eyes. "I'm sorry."

It was the reality of love. Her family needed her. Emily needed her. This town even needed her, and she couldn't just walk away because it would be easier. Love stood firm, even if it meant breaking her own heart in order to do so.

"Will you be all right?" Clarisse asked gently.

"I'll have to be," Lily said, sucking in a stabilizing breath.

Clarisse leaned forward and wrapped her arms around Lily, squeezing her close. The clock on the wall said 8:15, and outside the window, the sun was sinking lower and lower. She had to get her aunt to the church. There was no more time to gather information, and maybe Bryce had realized it was better to keep his distance from her, after all. Whatever happened, she'd have to trust this to God's hands, because she had nothing else in her arsenal.

Lord, if this marriage is wrong for Aunt Clarisse, please stop this wedding.

"You're going to be all right, Lily," her aunt said softly. "I know that for a fact. You're strong, sensible and smart. And we love you."

She had family, and that counted for a whole lot more than Bryce seemed to realize. That was enough of her own heartbreak—today was about Clarisse's wedding.

"We'll be late if we don't get moving," Lily said,

forcing herself to smile. "If you're absolutely sure about this…"

A radiant smile broke over Clarisse's face and she rose to her feet. "I've never been surer in my life."

Chapter Fifteen

Bryce had only noticed that his phone was dead when he tried to call Lily from the car on his way back to Comfort Creek. His friend had let him into the archives, and he'd found exactly what he was looking for—and more.

Fort Collins traffic was worse than he'd expected heading out of town on a Saturday. And now, as he approached Comfort Creek, the sun was low in the sky, and there were only a few minutes before that wedding started. If his cell phone had been charged, he'd have called her, but as it was his only option was to step on the gas and pray that he was on time. Timing mattered, because Aaron Bay was not who he claimed to be.

Hopefully, Chief Morgan would agree that his detour to Fort Collins had been necessary. He hadn't asked permission, because he hadn't wanted to take the chance on the chief denying it. Even now, with the information he'd garnered, he was only sure about one thing—Aaron Bay had a hidden past—but what that meant, he couldn't say. But Comfort Creek loved Clarisse Clifton, and Aaron had some explaining to do.

The church parking lot was so packed when he arrived that he was forced to park along the side of the road and walk the five hundred yards. The grassy lawn in front of the church was set up with folding chairs, the golden evening sunlight spilling over the grass.

Then Bryce saw Chief Morgan in full dress uniform. He was a guest for the wedding, too, it seemed, and the chief saw him at the same time. Bryce inwardly grimaced, then headed toward his temporary boss.

"Evening, Chief," Bryce said.

"You weren't on patrol." The other man didn't look amused, and he fixed him with an irritated stare.

"I was getting the information about Clarisse's husband-to-be," Bryce said, keeping his voice low. "I'm sorry for heading out like that, but I couldn't let them down."

"What did you find?" the chief asked.

Bryce gave a quick outline of his findings, and the chief nodded. "Go tell her now—before it's too late. We can discuss your extended sensitivity training later."

"Extended?" Bryce sighed. He'd known there would be consequences. "How long, sir?"

"I'll discuss it with your supervisor in Fort Collins on Monday." Chief Morgan nodded toward the church. "Clarisse is up there."

Many of the guests had already taken their seats, some still standing in groups chatting. A few kids ran in circles in the warm evening air. Bryce spotted Lily with her aunt on the church steps. Lily didn't see him at first, as he strode across the lawn toward them. She looked up only when his feet hit the cement sidewalk, and when she heard his footsteps, she turned and stared at him in surprise.

"Bryce?" Lily's face lit up at the sight of him.

"Hi." He'd never been more relieved to see someone in his life, but this wasn't about him and Lily, it was about Clarisse and her impending nuptials.

The smile slipped from Lily's face. "Is there…news?"

Clarisse turned toward him, her expression grim. She could sense it—he saw it in her face. He nodded slowly.

"We need to talk," he said.

"I'm getting married," Clarisse said firmly. "Can't this wait?"

"Not really," Bryce said. "I've come across a few things you'll need to know before you do this."

Clarisse's face paled, and her eyes flew across the church lawn to where her fiancé was talking with the minister. Aaron looked up and seemed to recognize something serious in Clarisse's expression, because he started toward them.

"Let's go inside where we can have some privacy," Bryce suggested.

A few minutes later, they all stood in the foyer of the church, Clarisse holding fast to Aaron's hand and Aaron looking uncomfortable. Lily looked up at Bryce, her expression taught and worried.

"Is it bad?" she whispered.

"I honestly don't know," Bryce replied softly. "We'll find out, I guess."

"Is there a problem?" Aaron asked.

"I think so," Bryce said. "I've done a little digging into your past, and you aren't who you claim to be."

Bryce pulled the copied documents out of his pocket and carefully unfolded them, then laid them on the welcoming table one by one. Lily stepped closer to look, her soft purple dress brushing against his pant leg.

Aaron sighed. "Clarisse knows everything."

Did she? He looked toward the older woman, and she wasn't betraying much in her expression. If she didn't know it all, she certainly deserved to.

"Your name isn't Aaron Bay," Bryce said. "You changed your name from Aaron Ventura eight years ago."

"Yes." Aaron nodded.

"Why?" Bryce asked. "That's why you have no paperwork trail—everything else is in the name you were born with. What are you hiding?"

Aaron was silent.

"You also have a sealed juvenile record," Bryce added. Bryce could very well have a record of his own right now, if it weren't for his father's intervention, so he knew the kinds of things that could be hidden.

Aaron closed his eyes for a moment, obviously trying to hold his temper.

"Just tell them," Clarisse said softly. "Or they'll worry themselves sick."

Aaron shrugged. "I was fourteen at the time. My father, Vic Ventura, was a violent man, and he used to beat up my mother on a regular basis. You can look up his police record, too, if you like. It's lengthy. I didn't know how to handle the abuse. My mother told me I had to keep it a secret, and so I never told anyone, and I knew I couldn't take him on and win that fight. But when he came home that night and started beating on my mother, something inside me snapped. I grabbed a rolling pin off the counter and I started to hit him." Aaron winced, then shook his head. "I'm not proud."

"And you got a criminal record from that?" Lily asked, frowning.

"I didn't *stop* hitting him…" Aaron's voice quavered. "I dropped the rolling pin and I started hitting him with my fists. I just couldn't stop. I nearly killed my father that night. He spent two months in the hospital recovering."

Bloody fists. Not stopping… Bryce shoved back his own memories.

"And once he did recover," Clarisse added, "Vic never raised a hand to his wife again."

"And I was charged with aggravated assault with a weapon. I pleaded guilty and spent two years in juvenile detention," Aaron concluded.

"And you changed your name to cover that up?" Bryce asked. "Because if you were protecting your mother—"

"Everyone remembered me," Aaron interrupted. "The thing is, my father's abusive ways weren't so secret. Everyone knew what he was doing, but my mother wouldn't press charges. But when I beat my father into a coma, no one saw a boy trying to rescue his mother from a lifetime of beatings, they only saw the violent son of a violent man. They all figured I was going to end up just like my old man."

The violent son of a violent man. Bryce had a similar reputation right now, and it stung. It didn't matter how far you ran, you couldn't get away from your parentage. He was the son of Richard Camden, and nothing would change that. He had that same walking potential.

"You could have just moved," Bryce said quietly. It was something Bryce had considered, too, but he'd discarded the idea as cowardly.

"I could have…" Aaron paused. "But it was more than that. Getting away from my past and from my father's taint on my life was more than a change of address, or even getting away from people who knew him. I had to change how I saw myself."

Clarisse slipped her hand into the crook of Aaron's arm, and Bryce glanced at Lily. She stood motionless, her hands clasped in front of her.

"I became a Christian ten years ago," Aaron went on. "And when I started fresh with God, I changed my name. I was thirty-two, and I wanted that fresh start to be complete. My father had a history of drug dealing, and I didn't want to be associated with all of that. That name change symbolized something more inside me, and I don't regret the decision."

"What about your mother?" Lily asked.

"She's out there on the lawn…waiting to see me get married."

Aaron's story did match the evidence, and Bryce had dug up a few of those original documents that corroborated it. A man running from his past, from the mistakes of his youth, from the tainted opinion of the people who knew him. He'd also seen Aaron's father's criminal record. Some days a complete break from it all was tempting, and Bryce could grudgingly identify.

"I knew all of this," Clarisse said quietly. "Aaron hasn't kept any secrets from me."

"I'm sorry, to both of you—" Lily began.

"What makes you so sure you aren't exactly like your father?" Bryce broke in.

"Bryce…" Clarisse began, but Aaron but his hand on her arm.

"It's all right," Aaron said. "It's better to have these

things in the open. I did agonize over that for a good many years. I listened to the opinions of the people who knew my family, and I thought they were right. But when I became a Christian, I discovered that there was one opinion that mattered more—God's. And when I read my Bible, it seems to me that God isn't as concerned with where we came from so much as where we're going. My past is just that—my past. I'm not my father, and I don't have to make his mistakes. When I chose God, God started working on me. I'm a new man—born again."

"Aren't you afraid of inherited weaknesses?" Bryce asked, his voice low.

"Oh, I inherited all sorts of weaknesses," Aaron said with a small smile. "But what I do with those is a choice. I might have had my father's temper, but I now have God's sense of justice, and that changes the direction of the anger. I'll never see a woman hurt again. God changes how I deal with fear and helplessness, too. Am I weak? Yes, but He's not, and I choose God." He turned toward Clarisse and smiled tenderly down into her eyes. "And I choose…her."

Clarisse's eyes welled with tears as Aaron bent down and pecked her lightly on the lips.

Bryce's mind was spinning. If Aaron Ventura could turn his life around and become a better man than his father had ever been… If God could take a man's weaknesses and weave them into something greater because of a choice to belong to his maker—

"Now." Clarisse sucked in a deep breath. "If we're all satisfied, I'm about to get married, and we planned this for sunset, so time is of the essence." She turned to Lily and smiled. "And as for you, dear girl, are you okay now?"

"I'm sorry, Auntie. I was worried. I thought—"

"Don't mention it again," Clarisse said softly. "I'll be just fine. And so will you."

They all moved toward the door. Lily slid her hand into the crook of Bryce's arm, and she tugged him closer and lifted his face toward him.

"I know you have to go—" She met his gaze pleadingly. "I just can't say goodbye like this. Stay for the wedding? Then we can say goodbye properly when it's over. I won't make it hard on you, I promise."

His goodbye wouldn't be quite as final as she thought, considering that he'd be given further sensitivity training, but this was worth it. He'd delivered what he promised, and he could deal with the humiliation of further punishment later. His mind was spinning with other thoughts, though.

"I'll stay for the ceremony," he assured her.

They came out of the church and down the wooden steps. A familiar baby's cry wavered across the lawn, and Bryce's gaze snapped to where Iris tried to soothe the infant. Lily sucked in a wavering breath.

"Looks like Emily missed me. I'll go get her."

I'm terrible with kids, Lord, he prayed silently. *Really terrible. Except for Piglet...*

The problem here was that he was in love—with both of them. And he didn't want to walk away, say goodbye, start over on his own back in Fort Collins. Reading his Bible, Bryce saw that Paul had championed the single life, but what if Bryce didn't want that life anymore? Jesus had made a whole new life possible. What if he wanted to be more like Joseph, and marry the woman he'd fallen in love with and be a step-dad to a baby who needed his protection?

Bryce went and had a brief word with Chief Morgan, and then he came to sit with Lily in the back row on the bride's side. Lily didn't want to disturb the ceremony if she needed to duck away with Emily if she started to fuss, but the baby was quiet in her arms, drinking a bottle with the earnest devotion she always gave to her food. Her little hands opened and shut with the rhythm of her drinking. Bryce reached over and stroked Emily's downy head with one finger, then let his hand drop.

This might be the last time she got to sit like this with Bryce, and she realized with a squeeze of her heart that she would miss him most desperately. Maybe God had sent Bryce for different reasons—for answers about Aaron, and perhaps to show her that she needed to be right here with her family, in Comfort Creek. But of all lessons in life, this one had stabbed deeper, hurt more.

The wedding was beautifully arranged. They'd set up candles at the end of each row of chairs, and at the front where the vows would be said. The combination of sunset and candlelight was warm and intimate—achingly perfect. Her heart was heavy as she watched the ceremony unfold. One day, she wanted this for herself, but it would have to be a day when she'd stopped longing for the man across from her to be Bryce.

Clarisse and Aaron stood holding hands at the front, the reds and pinks of sunset flooding over them. Clarisse's ivory dress looked pearly in the wash of lowering light. The minister was giving a little talk about love and marriage, and the life of togetherness that they could expect. It was a kind of love that Lily would have to wait a little longer to experience again...because healing her heart after Bryce was going to take time.

Her mother sat with all four boys near the front, and the twins were tugging at their new dress shirts uncomfortably. Randy and Burke were looking older—more grown-up than she'd ever seen them, and through her own sadness she felt a rush of pride. They'd be okay, too. Everyone who had told her to hang on because they would grow up eventually had been right. Kids grew, and kids made mistakes. They'd still need her, she knew, but maybe Randy and Burke could start settling down and then give her a hand with the twins. Was that anywhere in the near future? She could only hope. But there was another day tomorrow, and another day after that. They'd make it.

Clarisse and Aaron turned toward each other at the minister's request, and looked into each other's eyes.

"I, Clarisse, take you, Aaron, to be my lawfully wedded husband..."

Emily finished her bottle, and as Lily sat her up, the baby started to squirm. She needed to be burped, and as Lily reached down for a cloth to protect her shoulder, Bryce reached for the baby.

"Let me," he whispered.

Emily immediately calmed in his arms, and as Lily arranged the cloth over his shoulder, Bryce turned toward her, his face so close that he could have kissed her again. Heat rose in her cheeks at the thought, and she looked down at her lap. Those days were over, and she'd have to say a goodbye after this service with some semblance of dignity.

Emily had settled against Bryce's chest as he gently tapped her back.

"I wish this could last forever," Bryce murmured.

"I know you don't want to be a father," Lily whispered, "but you'd be wonderful at this."

She wasn't meaning to push, but he had to know how she saw him. He was silent for a moment, and he leaned toward her a little so that his muscled arm pressed against hers.

"If I could..." His voice was low and hesitant. "If I could be a good dad, would you be willing to be saddled with a lout like me?"

Tears misted her eyes. Her aunt was right that every man had something to deal with, and the more she thought about Clarisse and Aaron the more she realized that loving a man meant loving all of him, and being his strength just as often as he was hers. She couldn't leave Comfort Creek, no matter how desperately she'd miss Bryce once he was gone. But would she want him? She wanted him now—she wanted something that he couldn't give.

"I still have a family who needs me, Bryce."

"I'd stay."

His words were firm and resolute, and she turned toward him, her breath in her throat. Had she heard him right? But that didn't change what he wanted in life...

"But I thought you didn't want to be a father," she whispered. "And Emily—"

He reached over and took her hand in his firm grip and bent his head close to hers to keep their words private. "Aaron was right about having a choice. I thought I'd be a terrible father because my own dad was, but I do have a choice. I'm not my dad, either." He looked down at Emily, then back to Lily, and his voice broke when he spoke again. "I want this so badly it hurts."

"Does that mean—" She swallowed. "Do you mean—"

"It means I want this…you. I want to be with you for the rest of my life, and I want to help you take care of your brothers." Emily let out a soft burp, and he grinned down at the baby. "And Piglet, too. But most of all, Lily, I want a life with you."

"You mean you'll stay?"

"If you'll have me."

His words settled into her heart, and she found herself nodding before she'd even formed her answer. "Bryce, I will most definitely have you."

"But I want to get married, Lily. I want to do this in sickness and in health, for better or for worse. I want to help you wrangle your brothers and raise this little girl."

"Yes," she whispered, and a smile broke over his face and he was about to lean in and kiss her when the minister's joyful voice rang out, "What God has joined, let no man put asunder!"

Bryce pulled back with a wry smile, and a cheer went up as Clarisse and Aaron came down the aisle. The bride shot Lily an exuberant smile and she beamed back. She'd have news of her own soon, but she wouldn't take away from her aunt's special day. It could be their secret—for today at least—and she'd treasure all this happiness in her heart.

When the couple passed by, she felt a tap on her shoulder, and as she turned back toward Bryce, his lips came down onto hers in a soft and tender kiss. She put a hand on Emily's back and let her eyes flutter shut as the voices and bustle around her drifted away in the tender longing of that kiss and what had just happened settled into her heart.

"Lily?"

They pulled back to see Chris and Carson standing in the aisle, looking at them with uncertain expressions on their faces. Behind them, Burke and Randy were grinning, and her mother's face held an unspoken, but hopeful question.

"The wedding's over," Chris said, making a face. "In case you didn't notice."

Lily chuckled. "I want you all to come for breakfast tomorrow morning. I'm going to make a spread like you wouldn't believe."

"In honor of Aunt Clarisse and Uncle Aaron?" Carson asked.

"Them, too," she said. "I have news, and I won't be able to wait a moment longer than tomorrow morning."

"Hey, if Lily's cooking, we're there," Burke said, and Randy grunted his agreement.

This was her family—all of them—and Lily had never been so full of joy. When God said no, a heart could break, but when God said yes…

"I love you," Bryce said quietly into her ear.

"I love you, too."

Emily squirmed, and she took the baby back into her arms and leaned against Bryce's strong shoulder. When God said yes, a heart could fill so completely that it overflowed. A yes was worth the wait.

As they walked together across the church lawn, Bryce slipped an arm around her waist and tugged her closer. He paused, and when she looked up at him, his expression was worried.

"If I'm not very good at this—" he started.

"You're already rather good at this." She smiled up into his face.

"I'm serious," he said. "If I turn out to be insensitive or really bad at the kid thing, I want you to promise that you won't give up on me. You'll tell me how I can do better, and you'll stand by me. My mom kicked my dad out, and while he might have deserved it—"

She could see where that worry was coming from, and she let the smile fall from her lips. His home had fallen apart, and he was afraid of ending up just like his dad—out of the family circle.

"Then you promise me something, Bryce."

"Anything." She could tell by his expression that he meant that.

"Promise me that you'll try, even when it's hard, and even when it doesn't make sense to you—that you'll keep trying. That's all we need, you know. Someone who loves us enough to not give up."

"Always." His gaze softened again. "Trying—that's the easy part."

"I think we'll do just fine, Bryce."

Emily squirmed, and Bryce nodded toward the baby. "Can I take her?"

Lily laughed softly and handed Emily into his arms. "She already has you around her little finger, you know."

He looked down at Emily for a moment, then pressed a tender kiss on the top of her downy head, then he winked at Lily.

"I'm around your little finger, too," he said. "And speaking of fingers, you and I have some shopping to do…"

He loved her—she could see it in his eyes, and in

his eagerness to buy her a ring that would tell the world their plans. And she loved him—enough to help him learn how to do this right. She'd be Mrs. Camden, and for a while at least, the girls would outnumber the one man in the house. They'd baffle him with their feminine ways, she had no doubt, but she also knew that he'd love them with his whole heart.

And that would make their family just perfect.

* * * * *

If you enjoyed this story by Patricia Johns,
pick up these previous titles:

HIS UNEXPECTED FAMILY
THE RANCHER'S CITY GIRL
A FIREFIGHTER'S PROMISE
THE LAWMAN'S SURPRISE FAMILY

Available now from Love Inspired!

Find more great reads at www.LoveInspired.com

Dear Reader,

We receive all sorts of messages about who we are from society, from family, from media… Women are told what we're supposed to be. Be pretty, be cute, be quiet, be good. And when we don't live up to all those expectations, the message can get meaner. You're fat. You're ugly. You're unworthy. I found that when I finally pinpointed where those messages were coming from, they lost their power.

Everyone is going to have an opinion about you—that's an unfortunate fact—but there is only one opinion that matters, and that's God's. Never forget to whom you belong! It changes everything. And you are absolutely good enough. You're also beautiful and intentionally created.

If you'd like to connect with me, you can find me on my website at PatriciaJohnsRomance.com, or on Facebook. I'd love to meet you!

Patricia Johns

COMING NEXT MONTH FROM

Love Inspired®

Available July 18, 2017

A GROOM FOR RUBY

The Amish Matchmaker • by Emma Miller

Joseph Brenneman is instantly smitten when Ruby Plank stumbles—literally—into his arms. The shy mason sees all the wonderful things she offers the world. But with his mother insisting Ruby isn't good enough, and Ruby keeping a devastating secret, could they ever have a happily-ever-after?

SECOND CHANCE RANCHER

Bluebonnet Springs • by Brenda Minton

Returning to Bluebonnet Springs, Lucy Palermo is determined to reclaim her family ranch and take care of her younger sister. What she never expected was rancher neighbor Dane Scott and his adorable daughter—or that their friendship would have her dreaming of staying in their lives forever.

THE SOLDIER'S SECRET CHILD

Rescue River • by Lee Tobin McClain

Widow Lacey McPherson is ready to embrace the single life—until boy-next-door Vito D'Angelo returns with a foster son in tow. Now she's housing two guests and falling for the ex-soldier. But will the secret he's keeping ruin any chance at a future together?

REUNITING HIS FAMILY

by Jean C. Gordon

Released from prison after a wrongful charge, widowed dad Rhys Maddox wants nothing more than custody of his two sons. Yet volunteering at their former social worker Renee Delacroix's outreach program could give him a chance at more: creating a family.

TEXAS DADDY

Lone Star Legacy • by Jolene Navarro

Adrian De La Cruz is happy to see childhood crush Nikki Bergmann back in town and bonding with his daughter. But he quickly sees the danger of spending time together. With Nikki set on leaving Clear Water, could their wish for a wife and mother ever become reality?

THEIR RANCH REUNION

Rocky Mountain Heroes • by Mindy Obenhaus

Former high school sweethearts Andrew Stephens and Carly Wagner reunite when Andrew's late grandmother leaves them her house. At odds on what to do with the property, when a fire at Carly's inn forces the single mom and her daughter to move in, they begin to agree on one thing: they're meant to be together.

LOOK FOR THESE AND OTHER LOVE INSPIRED BOOKS WHEREVER BOOKS ARE SOLD, INCLUDING MOST BOOKSTORES, SUPERMARKETS, DISCOUNT STORES AND DRUGSTORES.

LICNM0717

Get 2 Free Books,
Plus 2 Free Gifts—
just for trying the Reader Service!

Love Inspired®

LI17R2

SPECIAL EXCERPT FROM

Love Inspired®

Ruby Plank comes to Seven Poplars to find a husband and soon literally stumbles into the arms of Joseph Brenneman. But will a secret threaten to keep them apart?

Read on for a sneak preview of
A GROOM FOR RUBY by **Emma Miller,**
available August 2017 from Love Inspired!

A young woman lay stretched out on a blanket, apparently lost in a book. But the most startling thing to Joseph was her hair. The woman's hair wasn't pinned up under a *kapp* or covered with a scarf. It rippled in a thick, shimmering mane down the back of her neck and over her shoulders nearly to her waist.

Joseph's mouth gaped. He clutched the bouquet of flowers so tightly between his hands that he distinctly heard several stems snap. He swallowed, unable to stop staring at her beautiful hair. It was brown, but brown in so many shades…tawny and russet, the color of shiny acorns in winter and the hue of ripe wheat. He'd intruded on a private moment, seen what he shouldn't. He should turn and walk away. But he couldn't.

"Hello," he stammered. "I'm sorry, I was looking for—"

"Ach!" The young woman rose on one elbow and twisted to face him. It was Ruby. Her eyes widened in surprise. "Joseph?"

"*Ya.* It's me."

Ruby sat up, dropping her paperback onto the blanket, pulling her knees up and tucking her feet under her skirt. "I was drying my hair," she said. "I washed it. I still had mud in it from last night."

Joseph grimaced. "Sorry."

"Everyone else went to Byler's store." She blushed. "But I stayed home. To wash my hair. What must you think of me without my *kapp*?"

She had a merry laugh, Joseph thought, a laugh as beautiful as she was. She was regarding him with definite interest. Her eyes were the shade of cinnamon splashed with swirls of chocolate. His mouth went dry.

She smiled encouragingly.

A dozen thoughts tumbled in his mind, but nothing seemed like the right thing to say. "I…I never know what to say to pretty girls," he admitted as he tore his gaze away from hers. "You must think I'm thickheaded." He shuffled his feet. "I'll come back another time when—"

"Who are those flowers for?" Ruby asked. "Did you bring them for Sara?"

"*Ne*, not Sara." Joseph's face grew hot. He tried to say, "I brought them for you," but again the words stuck in his throat. Dumbly, he held them out to her. It took every ounce of his courage not to turn and run.

Don't miss
A GROOM FOR RUBY
by Emma Miller, available August 2017 wherever
Love Inspired® books and ebooks are sold.

www.LoveInspired.com

LIEXP0717

Reward the book lover in you!

Earn points from all your Harlequin book purchases from wherever you shop.

Turn your points into *FREE BOOKS* of your choice
OR
EXCLUSIVE GIFTS from your favorite authors or series.

Join for FREE today at
www.HarlequinMyRewards.com.

Harlequin My Rewards is a free program (no fees) without any commitments or obligations.

MYR17

Love Inspired®

Inspirational Romance to Warm Your Heart and Soul

Join our social communities to connect with other readers who share your love!

Sign up for the Love Inspired newsletter at **www.LoveInspired.com** to be the first to find out about upcoming titles, special promotions and exclusive content.

CONNECT WITH US AT:

Harlequin.com/Community

 Facebook.com/LoveInspiredBooks

Twitter.com/LoveInspiredBks

LISOCIAL2017